THREE DAYS - BOOK SIX OF BEYOND THESE WALLS
A POST-APOCALYPTIC SURVIVAL THRILLER

MICHAEL ROBERTSON

EDITED AND COVER BY ...

To contact Michael, please email:
subscribers@michaelrobertson.co.uk

Edited by:

Pauline Nolet - http://www.paulinenolet.com

Cover design by Dusty Crosley

COPYRIGHT

Three Days - Book six of Beyond These Walls

Michael Robertson
© Michael Robertson 2020

Three Days - Book six of Beyond These Walls is a work of fiction. The characters, incidents, situations, and all dialogue are entirely a product of the author's imagination, or are used fictitiously and are not in any way representative of real people, places, or things.

Any resemblance to persons living or dead is entirely coincidental.

All rights reserved.

No part of this publication may be reproduced, stored in a retrieval system, or transmitted in any form or by any means electronic, mechanical, photocopying, recording, or otherwise, without the prior written permission of the author except in the case of brief quotations embodied in critical articles and reviews.

READER GROUP

Join my reader group for all my latest releases and special offers. You'll also receive these four FREE books. You can unsubscribe at any time.

Go to www.michaelrobertson.co.uk

THE ARENA
MICHAEL ROBERTSON

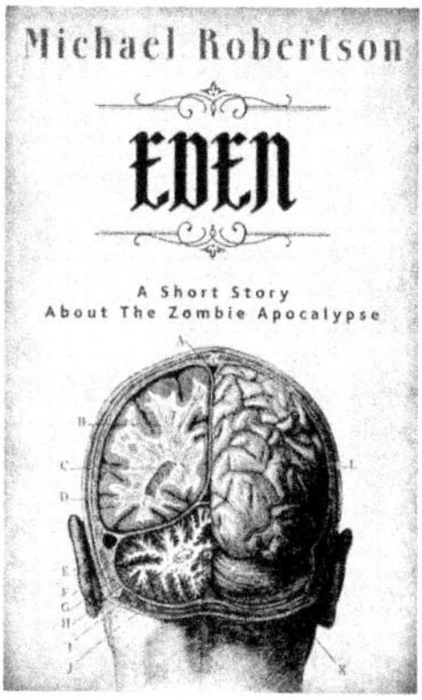
Michael Robertson
EDEN
A Short Story
About The Zombie Apocalypse

RAT RUN
A POST-APOCALYPTIC TALE
Michael Robertson

CHAPTER 1

The hard rain assaulted Olga, coming down on her as if nails were being fired from the clouds. It forced her to walk with a stoop, but at least she slowly sated her thirst, her tongue poked out to catch the muddy-tasting water. Her thin layer of clothes clung to her like a second skin, and she shivered from the biting cold, her muscles tense, cramps streaking up the side of her face from how hard she clamped her jaw. A hard kick to her lower back sent her stumbling several steps forwards. She pulled against her tight bonds, the rope wrapped around her wrists cutting into her skin. Her hands bound behind her back, she clenched them into fists and spoke through gritted teeth. "I'm walking! What more do you want from me?"

About six feet two inches tall, Carl had white hair and a fat face. Waxy skin with ruddy cheeks, his green eyes were stone cold in stark contrast to his wonky and yellow-toothed grin. He wore jeans and a shirt with a high collar that poked from the top of his sodden coat. The top few buttons of his shirt were undone, revealing scars similar to the ones Hawk had around his neck.

Matilda—her hands bound like Olga's—shoulder barged her friend to encourage her forwards. "He's just trying to get a reaction from you."

Olga took Matilda's guidance and moved on, but she wouldn't be silenced. "Maybe I *should* react. Show these pricks we can't be pushed around."

"I'm not sure that would send the correct message in our current state." Matilda shrugged as if to highlight her restricted mobility.

Peter—the other retired hunter tasked with taking them to Grandfather Jacks—walked beside Carl. Much shorter than the large angry man, he stood at around five feet and six inches and had skin as dark as William's. Different to Carl in almost every way, the most striking feature to mark him out resided in his compassionate face, his brown feline eyes glowing with a serenity absent from Carl's chaotic stare. This task clearly gave him little pleasure, and he spoke with a soft voice. "You might want to listen to your friend."

Like Olga should trust the good cop, bad cop routine. They were both horrible bastards. Forget that and she might as well walk herself to Grandfather Jacks. Aches ran across her gums when she bit down harder. A flick of her head to keep her hair from her face, Olga said, "Screw Max."

"Huh?" Matilda said.

"I can't stop thinking about what he's done. Screw him." Olga's pulse quickened and her breaths grew shallow. "He made me look like a fool in front of everyone."

"But—"

"Don't you dare excuse him."

"I wasn't going to, but how's thinking that way helping us right now? You should try to stay calm."

"How will being calm help?" Before Matilda could reply, Olga raised her voice. "The last thing I need is to be calm.

I'm going to be ready for war. What kind of ridiculous name is Grandfather Jacks anyway?"

Although Olga winced in anticipation of another kick from Carl, Peter's calm words met her question. "He's the High Father. The prophet. The only one amongst us who can commune with heaven."

"That sounds like bullshit to me. Besides, if there is a god, or High Father, or whatever you decide to call her, I'd say she left us a long time ago."

"*He*," Peter said.

"And you know that for a fact, do you?"

"In my heart." Peter drew a deep and calming breath as if feeling the presence of his god inside him. "Anyway, all will be revealed in time."

"You'll introduce me to the big man, will you?"

"We will all meet our maker in the end."

Already sodden, the long grass dragged on Olga's steps, seeds coating her soaked trousers. "That's a convenient way of avoiding the issue. You don't know the answers to any of life's big questions. None of us do. You might have faith in your convictions, and I might even be able to respect that should you choose to present them in that way, but to offer them as facts? You—" Olga's words were cut short by another shove. It sent her several paces forwards before she slammed down, her knees sinking into the muddy ground.

Another hard blow into the centre of her back, Olga fell face first into the grass. Fire ripped through her shoulder blades when Carl pulled her bound wrists, forcing her nose into the ground. Mud on her lips and in her mouth, she fought the urge to scream. *Don't give them the satisfaction.*

Peter positioned himself between Carl and Olga, forcing the sadistic guard to let go. He then lifted her to her feet, a hand beneath each armpit. "Now get up and shut up."

When Olga stood upright, Carl shoved Peter aside and kicked her a second time. She ran at the edge of her balance, tugging against her bonds until she finally fell again, face first onto the ground.

Squelching footsteps closed in on Olga. She rolled onto her back and lifted her knees. But Matilda prevented Carl from reaching her, shoulder barging him aside, so his kick hit thin air instead of the intended target of Olga's head.

For a second time Peter got between Carl and the girls and held his hands up as if to calm his fellow guard. "Think about what Grandfather Jacks will say if you beat these two black and blue."

His green eyes wide, his nostrils flared, Carl's barrel chest rose and fell with his heavy pants. He loomed over the smaller man. If he so desired, he'd overpower him in an instant. The rain had turned his thin white hair so damp it revealed his pink scalp beneath. "You think I give a shit about what he thinks?"

Adrenaline surged through Olga as she got to her feet and shivered, awaiting Carl's next outburst.

A gentler shove, Peter encouraged Olga forwards. "Move before this situation gets away from all of us."

A nauseating clamp to her stomach as they set off again, Olga spoke so only Matilda heard. "I promise you, before these clowns can deliver us to Grandfather Jacks, I'm going to cut both their throats."

"And if the moment comes, I'll be right beside you." Her brown eyes calm, Matilda said, "But for now, we have to accept they're the ones in control. Besides, we don't know what's happening with the boys."

"Are you saying we should wait to be rescued? Firstly, how the hell will they know where we are? It would be quite a lucky guess for them to find us.

Secondly, I'm no damsel in distress. I plan on getting *myself* out of this."

"I'm saying we should pick our moment, and it isn't now."

"Less talking, more walking," Carl said. "You two don't know how lucky you are, let me tell you."

"Don't," Matilda said, catching Olga's reply before it left her mouth.

Carl continued. "I've heard what some of the hunters do with their hostages before delivering them to Grandfather Jacks."

"But we're not those types of guards." Although Peter aimed his words at the girls, he clearly meant them for Carl. The deep-voiced sadist grumbled an indecipherable response to his friend. Hopefully an acceptance. Olga hated the fact, but Matilda was right. The odds were not in their favour.

Olga breathed through her nose and shook her head. "I will wait for the right moment, but I swear, they will die at my hand."

"What's that, little one?" Carl said.

Matilda stepped closer to Olga. "And I'll be at your side when the moment's right."

The meadow stretched out ahead of them, the wind controlling the long grass. Olga's eyes stung with tiredness, grief, and the glow of the rising sun as it found gaps in the grey clouds.

Olga might have let it go, but Carl clearly hadn't. Even though she refused to look at the vile man, she heard the grin in his voice. "Come on, little one. Surely you have more fight in you? Tell me all your complaints so I can forward them to the 'I don't give a shit' department."

A surge of adrenaline turned Olga's pulse into a bass drum. She spun and charged Carl. The man might have been twice her size and have full use of his fists, but he didn't have her spirit. He smiled and dropped into a crouch, his hands balled.

The squelch of Matilda's steps joined Olga's as she joined the attack.

Spirit or not, Carl moved fast. The air left Olga's lungs. The first she knew of the blow was when it hit her stomach. Her feet lifted from the ground as she wrapped around his clenched fist. She turned weightless and flew backwards, landing bottom first with a squelch, her diaphragm locked in violent spasms.

Despite gasping for breath, Olga tried to sit up as Carl landed a right cross on Matilda's chin with a *crack!* Her friend's legs turned bandy and she crumpled.

Close to vomiting, Olga rolled forwards while Carl punched the already unconscious Matilda again. "Stop!" Olga gasped, unable to get her words out because of her need to breathe. "Stop!"

Carl kicked Matilda in the stomach, flipping her onto her back.

"Leave—" Olga got up onto one knee "—her."

Peter grabbed Carl across his chest and pulled him back.

Olga stood up, still fighting for breath. "Leave her alone, you prick." She charged Carl yet again. This time she read his attack and stepped aside, evading his blow. As the man pulled back, she jumped like a salmon, a white flash bursting through her vision when she headbutted him.

Fury glowed in Carl's glare, but before he could get to Olga, Peter stepped between them again and pushed the guard back. "Grandfather Jacks will hang us out to dry."

"I don't care!"

"I do, so stop it!"

Although Carl finally stepped back and some of the

tension left his frame, he remained fixed on Olga, his shoulders rising and falling with his ragged breaths.

A stinging throb where her forehead had met Carl's nose, Olga stumbled back several steps from Peter's hard shove. She ground her teeth and remained fixed on Carl, his top lip coated with blood. Let him come at her again. See what happened.

Too fast for Peter to react, Carl sidestepped his partner and kicked Matilda in the chin. Her head snapped back. As Peter went to Matilda, Carl charged Olga. "You won't get me twice, you little shit."

A flash from where Carl punched her. Her sinuses on fire. Olga's legs gave out and her world turned dark.

CHAPTER 2

The long and sodden grass whipped William's legs as he jogged through it. Cyrus, the slowest of the pack and least able to defend himself, ran in the middle of the group, dictating their pace. And of course William had thought about leaving him, but at least he hadn't said it aloud. Max took the lead ahead of Cyrus, mainly because he seemed to want to be on his own, and Artan ran behind William. The lashing rain and boggy ground made Cyrus even slower. How much of a lead did the girls have on them already, and was it growing because of their pathetic pace?

As Cyrus slowed down in front of him, William clamped his jaw, held Jezebel with just one hand, and shoved him in the back.

Cyrus stumbled, his arms windmilling as he fought to keep his balance. William growled at him through clenched teeth, "Keep running."

Cyrus nodded several times as if trying to convince himself more than anyone else. He ran like he walked, his gait awkward as if his feet were too large for him to control. He stretched his mouth wide as he fought for breath.

Less than a minute had passed and Cyrus' steps grew clumsier as his pace slowed again. Before William could shove him for a second time, Artan said, "Let him rest."

"You think we have time for that?"

"What other choice do we have? We're a team, remember?"

"Tell that to Max."

If Max heard him, he hid it well. The mood had turned darker since they'd found out what had happened to the girls. Sure, William could have managed himself better and maybe been more civil, but none of them had gone as dark as Max.

"Max," Artan said, "we're taking a break."

Max let his arms fall at his sides, slowing to a halt before facing the sky and opening his mouth to let nature quench his thirst.

"Jesus," William muttered, slowing down a few steps after the others. He too sated his dry throat with the downpour. He spun Jezebel in his two-handed grip so the wide double-bladed head turned. His chest tight, he tried to regulate his breaths to slow his pulse. They didn't have time to rest.

The rainclouds had blocked the sun for most of the day, the dark grey turning darker as they edged closer to evening. The long grass in the meadow swayed, a gust of wind hitting William so hard he stumbled a step to the left. For the briefest moment, it felt like his strength might abandon him.

Artan sidled over to William and spoke beneath his breath. "Go easy on Cyrus, yeah? He's not as fit as you or I. And truth be told, we all need the rest. We've been running for the past hour." Of the four of them, Artan appeared to need the break the least. His skin only damp because of the rain, his breaths even.

"But we don't have time," William said. "You heard Mary

and Rita. They said it'll take a couple of days to get to Grandfather Jacks' community."

"And we have three until the full moon."

Both Max and Cyrus joined them, both of them panting from the run. "What if Grandfather Jacks chooses his bride sooner?" William said.

Artan shrugged. "We don't know for sure, but if we've learned anything from our time in Umbriel, it's that Grandfather Jacks loves routine and ceremony. Why would that change now? As far as they're concerned, we've been given to Magma. They won't be expecting us, so it makes little sense that they'd break their routine."

"But what if the girls think we're not coming? How can you be so calm?"

"You'd prefer it if I shouted and ranted?"

For the past few seconds, Cyrus had stood with his mouth stretched wide while he faced the sky. The rain had gathered in his mouth, and it now sounded like a filling cup. William said, "Jesus! Will you just swallow that? It's like hanging out with a damn child."

Cyrus gulped the water.

William clamped his jaw and turned his back on the group. They'd get nothing from arguing with one another.

Artan handed his war hammer to Cyrus and took Ranger's sword from the boy.

"What am I supposed to do with this?" Cyrus said.

William tutted and shook Jezebel while holding the axe with both hands. "You swing it!"

Although Artan paused for a moment and fixed on William, he let it slide. He then waded through the long grass to a nearby tree, reached up, and tugged on one of the thick branches. It came free with the crack of splintering wood. He stabbed the sword into the damp ground before holding the branch with both hands and snapping it over his knee. The remainder of the branch now about five feet long, the thickness consistent all the way down, he closed one eye and looked along the shaft, turning it to inspect its straightness. All the while, William's breath slowed as he took the time for a well-needed recovery. Maybe they did all need a break.

Artan used Cyrus' sword to whittle a point, and William shook his head. "You can't be serious."

"What?" Artan said.

"A spear? That makes us as bad as them."

"No, oppressing women and handing them over to some crazed leader makes us as bad as them. Copying their very effective weaponry makes us smart."

William snorted. "You think?"

"It seems like all you want to do is argue. I've really not got the energy for it. Spears are effective out here. Besides, you've already proven you won't listen to reason."

Cyrus stepped between them. "Will you two just leave it?"

But William moved around him, edging closer to Artan. "Go on then!"

Artan pulled his head back. "Go on then what?"

"Say it."

"I already have."

"No, not in a passive-aggressive, whining-little-kid way. You've clearly got something you want to get off your chest, so say what you feel."

"You want me to spell it out?" Artan said. "Fine. I told you Samson was a wrong'un, but you didn't listen. I told you Umbriel wasn't a good place, but you didn't listen. And now I want to use a spear to give ourselves a better chance of surviving this run, you still won't listen. I've not said anything before now because on the whole you've made good decisions."

"You think it's a bad choice for me to want us to keep running after the girls?"

"Look at yourself."

Rocking with his ragged breaths, William's pulse still slammed through him.

"*I* could carry on," Artan said. "*I* could run for another few hours, but it's not just Cyrus who needs a rest. So let me make this spear while we're all catching our breath, yeah?"

William sneered. "Carrying that thing makes us as bad as them."

Artan's nose wrinkled and his expression twisted. He threw the now sharpened branch at William. The shaft flew past his face, missing him by about a foot.

Had Max and Cyrus not gasped when they spun around, William would have remained fixed on Artan. Instead, he took in the diseased, now on its back, a spear protruding from its face like a flagpole. Its left leg twitched as the life left it.

William pulled his shoulders back and raised his chest when Artan approached. The boy handed Cyrus his sword back and took his war hammer. Tense in anticipation of Artan slamming into him, William leaned into the contact, but Artan turned sideways, passing him as he raised his hammer and brought it down on the head of the creature with a blow strong enough to bury a fencepost.

The wind howled, the rain lashing down, the grass swaying around them. "I'm sorry." William hung his head. "I can't cope with the stress of being separated from them."

Artan paused from cleaning the end of his spear in the grass.

William's lips buckled and he had to cough to clear the lump from his throat. "I'm so scared for Matilda and Olga."

The frown on Artan's brow softened and he nodded. "We all are. But we need to be sensible and make sure we don't kill ourselves while trying to get to them."

William nodded several times. "I need to manage myself better. And I need to listen to you more."

"I'm not that little kid you once knew."

"I know. I'm sorry. And I'm sorry, Cyrus. I owe you my life for how you let us pass in the national service area."

Artan pulled William into a close hug. "We all want the same thing. We'll get the girls away from Grandfather Jacks, I promise."

His eyes stinging with exhaustion and grief, William nodded.

Cyrus rubbed his back. "We're in this together. We'll make sure they're okay."

William cleared his throat again. "Right, if you're all rested, can I suggest we get moving again?" When none of the others protested, William set off at a slower pace than before, the rain stinging as it continued to hammer down on them, the strong winds chilling him to his core.

CHAPTER 3

Fire in her sinuses, her forehead stinging from where she'd headbutted Carl, Olga opened her eyes. She still lay in the long damp grass, Carl's twisted and ruddy face peering down on her. His fists balled, he panted, his thick frame rising and falling. Deep lines scored his furrowed brow. His eyes had lost focus.

Olga couldn't have been out for longer than a few seconds. Her head pounded and the coppery taste of her own blood coated the back of her throat. She rolled onto her front and slowly got to her knees without the use of her bound hands. A deep sniff filled her mouth with a rubbery clot. Her stomach bucked and she spat it into the long grass. Carl stepped back as more claret dripped from her nose and ran over her top lip. Unable to wipe it away, she looked up into the lashing rain.

As Carl moved back another pace, Olga relaxed … until Peter approached. He'd pretended to be the nice one of the two, but what did they have planned for the girls? She shook her head and said, "Stay the hell away from me. I will fight you both again. And this time, you'll have to kill me to stop me."

Peter raised his hands in defence. "*I* don't want to hurt you. I just—"

"How dare you even think about telling us what to do?" Carl stepped across the front of Peter and closer to her, his teeth bared, his breaths heavy and irregular. "You're our prisoners. We own you." As he said it, he looked her up and down, her sodden clothes leaving little to the imagination. "*We* call the shots. You'd do well to remember that."

The skin at the base of Olga's neck tightened, and she fought to suppress a shudder. This man's rage ran deep. Rooted in something buried inside him, it yearned for release. It sought to destroy. Matilda still lay in the grass from where he'd knocked her over. If Olga backed down now, they might think they could do whatever they wanted to them. She needed to sow doubt in them at the very least. "You won't beat me."

Carl stepped another pace closer. So close Olga could smell the stale sweat on his body. Even with the downpour, he stank as if his toxic masculinity oozed from him.

"You come near me with that thing"—Olga nodded in the direction of his crotch—"and I swear I'll make you pay. I *refuse* to lie down. I will not play your little games. You'll have to kill me before I let that happen."

For the second time in as many minutes, Carl moved quicker than Olga could track. As he passed her, his thick arm caught her around the neck and he tightened his grip.

Olga wheezed and kicked her feet when Carl lifted her from the ground.

Carl's right arm bulged and his panting breaths tickled her ear. He sprayed spittle across the side of her face. "You think I'm some kind of rapist?"

Her throat too restricted to reply, her bound hands wriggled with a need to pull his arm away.

Carl squeezed even tighter, the blood pressure swelling through her head, her pulse pounding in her temples. "You need to learn when to wind your neck in."

"Put her down!" Matilda remained on the ground, but she'd now sat up. Her chin was red from where Carl had attacked her, her hair dishevelled.

Peter stepped towards Carl, genuine worry creasing his features. But he halted with the shrill and demented cry of nearby diseased.

Olga hit the ground hard when Carl released his grip. Her hands still bound behind her back, she leaned forwards and gulped hungry gasps of air.

Peter and Carl now stood side by side, drew their spears, and faced the diseased.

Her head spinning, it took for Olga to see which way the men faced to know where the diseased came from. The swish of the long grass preceded three of the vile creatures. Slashing arms, torn faces, necrotised flesh. Long scraggly hair on wrinkled scalps. One woman and two men.

Carl had already revealed his speed, but Peter now moved quicker, loosing his spear faster than Olga could track it. It embedded in the face of one of the male diseased, burst from the back of his skull, and dropped him mid-run. Despite having another spear, Peter drew his long knife. Save the second spear for hunting. Don't contaminate it unless they had to.

But Carl hadn't thrown his first one yet.

Snarling, snapping, thrashing … the two remaining diseased were just metres away. Peter widened his stance while Carl threw down his weapons.

"What the hell?" Olga said.

Carl charged and used his forearm to knock the female diseased to the ground. Her ratty black hair flew wide in a flourish as she fell. Peter jumped on her and buried his knife into the side of her head. The familiar pop of a skull gave way to brute force.

The male diseased followed Carl's path, the tall man back on his feet as he moved several steps to the left. The man might have been batshit crazy, but he clearly had enough faculties to not drag Peter into his insanity. Olga's jaw fell loose when Carl punched the diseased. His right fist met the creature's chin, its momentum sending it stumbling past him on his left.

The diseased shook its head, its long and wet scraggly hair swishing. It gnashed its teeth, screamed, and charged again. But a sound worse than the fury of a diseased drowned it out. Wild and uninhibited. Erratic and shrill. Carl laughed.

On the second charge, Carl lowered himself before leaping into the air and kicking the creature in the centre of its chest. He moved fast for a big man. The beast wheezed like an old set of bagpipes as it fell back into the long grass. Where any sane person would have taken the creature's fall as a chance to end it, Carl laughed harder and waited.

The beast stumbled to its feet and charged again, its gait even more unsteady. For the third time, Carl landed a blow, an uppercut driven into the creature's chin. It connected with a hard *clop!*

Several paces past him, the diseased fell face first into the long grass. Olga breathed in time with Carl, panting in unison with the man, who waited. But the diseased didn't get back up again.

Carl approached the defeated creature with slow and steady steps. The same lust in his eyes as when he'd leaned over Olga. A wide smile spread into a rictus grin, his eyes were bloodshot as tears ran down his cheeks. His brow furrowed, his eyebrows pinched in the centre, he gnashed his jaw as if savouring the taste of his victory.

Over the beast, Carl froze and fixed on the thing as if he pitied it. He then lifted his leg. His grin fell as he clamped his jaw tight before he stamped on the beast's head. It popped, a sharp spasm snapping through both its legs before they fell limp.

Carl stamped on it again. And again. And again. The ground squelched. "You fuck! You fucking fuck! You won't do that to me again. You won't."

Matilda had now gotten to her feet and stepped closer to Olga. Peter moved across in front of the two girls as the first line of defence should the crazed Carl turn his attention their way again.

The day turned colder, Olga's damp clothes clinging to her. At least five minutes passed before Carl finally stopped attacking the dead creature. Now done, he slowly turned to the others, his face alive with malice.

"You're finished now, Carl," Peter said. "We're all done. We need to move on. You must feel a bit better?"

Carl nodded, although his dead eyes gave nothing away.

"Good. Now hold back for a while. Give yourself the time you need to get your head straight, yeah?"

"I feel better." The low voice bubbling from Carl's throat didn't belong to the man. It seemed to come from deeper inside him. From one of the demons he'd pushed to the bottom of his being.

Olga stepped back a pace. For the second time, the skin at the base of her neck crawled.

"That's good to hear, buddy," Peter said, the *crack* of his hand patting Carl's damp back. Uncertainty clung to his words, the air between him and his friend palpable with simmering tension. The dark storm clouds above them rolled with the threat of a thunderstorm. After a pause, Peter nodded at Carl, clearly giving him a moment to object. When he didn't, he led the girls away.

At least twenty metres between them and Carl, Peter said, "I don't want to hurt you."

Olga snarled. "He does though."

"He's a complicated character."

"You reckon? What kind of lunatic fights the diseased with their bare fists?"

"The kind of lunatic who needs a release. Now you might want to keep your voice down."

Matilda nudged Olga and flicked her head back. "Just give the man some time to calm down, yeah?"

"Besides," Peter said, "Carl's been on the other side of the funnel. He's been farther south than I have. He's dealt with hordes. Before this journey's done, you'll be glad to have him at your side."

"What's the funnel?" Olga said. "And what do you mean *he's been farther south*?"

"You'll find out. Not about going farther south. Fortunately for you, Grandfather Jacks' community isn't too far past the funnel. But my point is, while the diseased are similar on both sides, there are far more of them in the south, and they hunt in packs."

Carl had made up some ground on them, which Matilda showed Olga by shoving her again and nodding behind. The man stalked them, a crazed hunter toying with his prey.

Peter's eyes betrayed little when he looked back at his friend. "I'll say it again; neither of us want to hurt you. We're not who you should fight."

"So Grandfather Jacks is?"

Peter shook his head. "No. Of course not. My point is,

you should pick your battles. Your rage will get you in trouble. Learn from your friend. Know when to keep your mouth shut. All you're doing at the moment is poking the bear. There's little you can do right now, especially with your hands tied behind your backs. Acceptance will be your salvation."

"Subservience more like."

Peter let the comment go.

After Peter had opened up a slight lead on them, Matilda spoke so only Olga heard her. "I think he's right. I don't trust him, but we need to wait for the right time to get out of this mess. If we keep him"—she nodded at Peter—"onside, we'll get them both to lower their guard eventually."

"So we let these men control and oppress us, and who knows what else they might do?"

"We need to find a way out of this," Matilda said, "but if we fight everything put in front of us, we won't have the energy to fight what we most need to rail against. I can't keep on taking kickings like the one I just got and be ready when the time's right."

"If neither of you want to hurt us," Olga called to Peter, "then why don't you let us go? Or release our bonds at least?"

"We can't do that."

"But handing us over to Grandfather Jacks *is* hurting us."

Peter drew a water flask from his belt. A small bottle carved from wood, he removed the stopper with a slight *pop* and took a sip from it before slowing down to hold it to Matilda's lips. After she'd drank from it, he did the same for Olga. Her thirst quenched, she copied Matilda in poking her tongue out for a strip of dried deer meat. Her mouth watered as the salt spread across her tongue and her stomach rumbled.

"Let's try not to fall out, yeah?" Peter said.

Matilda nodded.

Maybe her friend did have a point. Maybe Peter didn't want to harm them. And maybe he wanted to believe in them so desperately that he'd lower his guard. Maybe he'd give them the opening they needed to get the hell away before they were delivered to Grandfather Jacks. For now, Olga just needed to make sure she kept her wits so she had the presence of mind to see the moment when it came.

CHAPTER 4

The sun might have been weak that day, but William had held out some hope the rain might stop and his clothes would have a chance to dry. No such luck. As day transitioned into night, the rain continued to fall and the sharp wind cut through him with surgical precision. Another reason to keep moving. They might have slowed their pace, but he led the line, pulling the others along at a fast march. He wouldn't stop until they reached the girls.

The group moved with squelching steps, the moon mocking them when it appeared from behind the fast-moving clouds every few minutes. Close to full, it shone as a spotlight. It reminded them that in just three days, it would be time for Grandfather Jacks to pick his brides.

Artan quickened his pace and fell into step beside William. "We need to rest at some point. How many times are we going to have to say that to you?"

"This is a better pace though, right? And what will resting do to us with these damp clothes?"

"It's less about the rest and more the fact that we can't *see* anything." They'd entered a small abandoned town and were surrounded by ruined buildings no taller than one to two storeys. Artan ran a sweeping arm in front of himself as if showing their surroundings to William for the first time. "In a place like this, we can get ambushed from anywhere during daylight. It's a million times worse now. What use are we to the girls if we die before we get to them?"

"What use are we if we get pneumonia? Just a little bit longer, yeah?"

Artan shook his head. "You've said that several times already. How *long* is a little bit longer?"

"What if we catch up to them?"

"You think we'll catch them? The retired hunters know the way. We don't. We'd have to be incredibly lucky to pick the most direct route, and I'm not prepared to risk everyone's life on luck."

"I'd rather rely on luck than risk letting a good woman like your sister die."

The moon lit Artan's face, the familial resemblance turning a sharp twist through William's heart. The boy's jaw widened from where he clamped it and shook his head. Matilda had stared similar disdain at him in the past. The boy dropped back to be with the others.

Several more paces and William stopped in his tracks. A canted silhouette shuffled from behind a building. It halted and swayed where it stood, the moonlight at its back, its face in shadow.

William tightened his grip on Jezebel.

"Oh, shit," Cyrus said.

The creature threw its arms in the air. Its cry ricochetted off the ruined buildings as it charged.

William twisted his planted feet in the soggy ground, his boots sodden, his feet swollen inside his damp socks. The beast stumbled through the long grass, a wild animal closing the gap between them.

With Jezebel wound back, William waited. He then met the creature with a full-bodied swing, warm blood spraying his front as he buried the axe into the beast's shoulder.

The diseased yelled louder than before and fell, writhing on the ground but unable to avoid the heavy blow of Artan's war hammer. A deep *crack* and the creature fell still. Artan pointed down at it. "*This* is why we need to find somewhere to rest. We can't possibly fight these things in the—"

More screams cut him off.

William turned on the spot.

They came at them from all sides. A large cloud passed across the moon, turning the abandoned town darker.

"Take this." Artan handed his spear to the weaponless Max. "It's useless at long range if I can't see them. Use it to take them down when they get near."

What little light that pushed through the clouds shone on Cyrus' sword from where it shook in his grip. The boy turned left and right, responding to every echo. And why wouldn't he? "Where are they coming from?" William said.

A similar turn from one side to the other, but more measured than Cyrus, Artan shook his head. "I don't know." Slathering breaths. Heavy steps. "But they're getting closer."

Max moved off in one direction, but Artan reached out to him and dragged him back. "We don't know where they're coming from. Stay with us. We're stronger together."

Squelching steps from several angles. They were getting closer. Ten of them? Twenty? Hard to tell.

Cyrus sobbed. "I'm no good at this."

His shoulders squared, his war hammer raised and ready to use, Artan stood alert. "Get ready."

William turned to where the first diseased had come from. The steps were quieter in that direction.

"Diseased!" Max charged forward to meet several creatures bursting from behind one of the buildings.

Twice as many came from around the other side of the wrecked house. Artan darted towards them.

Several appeared on William's left. Too dark to be sure how many.

The *crunch* of Artan's attack spurred on William, who swung Jezebel at a silhouette. The *crack* of the axe head sank into one of the creatures' skulls. He pulled her back out and swung at the next one, jumping aside to avoid several more on the charge.

The diseased pack turned around and came at him again. More appeared from behind another ruined building. William stepped back onto a small rock. His ankle buckled beneath him and he fell. A diseased flew over the top of him, grabbing thin air where he'd been moments before. He pulled Jezebel into his chest and rolled away. Four to five diseased dived on the spot he'd vacated. Jumping up, he slammed the blade into the back of a creature's head.

A yell that burned his throat, the screams of diseased all around, William spun on the spot, swinging Jezebel out around him. Not all of the creatures went down, but every time he caught one, his attack pushed them away.

Dizzy, gasping for breath, and sweating, William slowed down when Jezebel stopped making contact with the diseased. The boy with the war hammer in front of him, the boy with the spear to his left, William said, "That's all of them?"

Artan panted, his shoulders hunched as he gripped his weapon with both hands and scanned their surroundings. "I told you we should have found somewhere to rest up. How the hell are we supposed to fight diseased in the dark? You're going to get us all killed, William."

"Uh," Max said, turning one way and then the other, "where's Cyrus?"

The tension left Artan's frame as he too turned on the spot. "Cyrus?"

William winced in anticipation of another blasting that didn't come. Instead, Artan called the boy's name several more times before his frame sagged. "If I shout any louder," Artan said, "I'll bring more diseased down on us."

"W-where do you think he is?" William said.

Artan's voice cracked with his restrained grief. "Well, I doubt he's decided now's a good time to play hide-and-seek."

Max remained alert, Artan's spear in his grip.

"So what do we do?" William said.

"What we should have done an hour or two ago." Artan walked at William, slamming his shoulder into him on his way past. He reached one of the taller ruined buildings and climbed.

Three floors, the first two intact, William followed after him. "You sure you want to rest up here?"

Artan spun on William. "How about you shut up, yeah? All you've done today is put us all in danger and possibly killed Cyrus. I think the best thing you can do right now is keep quiet, because if you don't, I won't be responsible for my actions. The plan is for us to wait until first light so we can check every one of these bodies for Cyrus. If he's not amongst the dead, then we widen our search. I'm not giving up on him until I know he's gone."

But what about Matilda? What if Cyrus had run off? William kept his thoughts to himself. Artan had every right to be pissed.

Artan and Max walked over to a window on the first floor

and stared out. When William joined them, he nodded into the darkness. "How long do you think it'll take to get to Grandfather Jacks?"

"Who knows?" Artan said. "We need to find Cyrus first." He shoved William aside as he moved to a shadowy corner of the building.

Max turned and found another corner, his mood as dark as it had been since they'd left Umbriel.

One more corner remained. The space where the fourth and final one should have been now sat exposed from where the wall had collapsed. William skulked over to it and sat on his own. The shape of the building funnelled the wind straight into him. Shivering, cold, and alone. When the morning came, it would get worse. It would shine a spotlight on his foolishness. The open accusation for Cyrus' death would be much harder to avoid in the cold light of day.

CHAPTER 5

Every sound snapped Olga rigid as she turned to the left and right in a desperate attempt to locate each source. Where the night had taken away their ability to see the diseased, she had to rely on her other senses to give her an early warning.

The moon hung high above them. Nearly full, its silver glow highlighted their environment for short bursts before the dark clouds swept in front of it, burying it for minutes at a time. It left them surrounded with no more than silhouettes of the ruined structures that had once served a purpose in a forgotten life.

The rain had stopped several hours previously, but Olga's clothes were still damp. She shivered in the strong wind, her jaw aching from her tight clench against the icy blast. Her thighs stung from where the thick fabric of her trousers chafed.

Olga walked on tired legs, the boggy ground sapping her energy. She breathed through her mouth, her nose still clogged from where Carl had bloodied it. Although, the tentative and wobbly steps of Matilda told her she'd gotten away lightly. Since she'd been kicked in the head, she'd not had anything to say for herself.

Carl remained at least twenty feet behind them. So far back his tall and thick frame and canted stance painted a demented silhouette. A madman lost in the darkness. And thank god they couldn't see his face. Although maybe imagining what it looked like was worse. A switch had flicked in him since Olga's headbutt. He now maintained a safe distance as if it were the only way to contain the crazy.

A step closer to Matilda, which also meant a step farther away from Peter, who walked much closer to them than his larger friend, Olga kept her voice low. "Surely we've got to stop soon? And when we do, how will we keep an eye on Carl? I won't be able to sleep with him nearby."

Matilda stumbled on the uneven ground, wincing from the action as her hair fell across her face. Both hers and Olga's hands still bound, she stuck out her bottom lip and blew up at her fringe. When the hair didn't move, she flicked her head to one side. "I think Peter will keep him away."

Although closer to them than Carl, Peter still walked at least fifteen feet ahead of the girls. If he heard them, he hid it well. "You think we can trust him?"

"We have a choice?"

Olga shrugged. "There's always a choice."

"Not now." Matilda shook her head. "Not at this moment."

"There won't ever be a perfect time. And what if we run into more diseased?"

"I don't think the diseased are our biggest threat."

As if on cue, Carl spat and hissed like an angry badger. He shook his head and muttered to himself, throwing air punches with his large fists. Olga's shoulders tensed, her body twisting. If she charged him now, could she end him?

But Matilda had already taken a beating because of her actions. She couldn't let that happen again. "I hope Peter has a plan."

Matilda sighed. "Me too."

"Do you really think the boys are okay?" Olga said.

"Whatever doubt I have in my mind, I need to recognise it doesn't serve me. Besides, I truly believe I can feel them. My instinct tells me they're still alive."

"Although Max can do one. I don't care about him. What a prick to do that to me in front of everyone."

"Surely you get why he behaved that way?"

"What do you mean?" Olga stopped, although when Carl didn't, she moved on again. "What's William told you?"

"It's not what he's told me." Matilda had also continued walking. "It's pretty obvious when you think about it." After throwing a glance at the much smaller Peter ahead of them, Matilda stepped closer. "Think about his ... powers."

"What's that got to do with anything?"

"Everything." Another step closer, Matilda said, "He's probably a ..."

Peter's head turned as he angled an ear back their way.

Even quieter than before, Matilda said, "... carrier. So if you and him ..." She raised her eyebrows.

"Oh shit!"

Peter spun to face them.

Heat flushed Olga's cheeks and her heart pounded. What the fuck did the nosy old bastard want? What did their conversation have to do with him? Even with her hands bound, she'd kick his arse. No taller than her and probably nowhere near as strong. Although definitely the kinder of the two guards, they probably didn't want to be upsetting him too.

Peter set off again.

"I've been such a dick," Olga said. "Why did I kiss Hawk? What if they're not okay? What if the last thing Max ever saw of me was that? What then?"

"I believe they're okay."

"Hardly concrete though, is it?"

"If it's proof you're looking for, I'm afraid I can't give it to you. I'm just doing what I can to remain sane."

"We need to find them," Olga said. "I need to make it up to Max."

On Matilda's next step, she stumbled, dragging air in through clenched teeth.

"Are you still sore from what Carl did to you?"

While leaning forwards, bent at the waist, Matilda nodded.

"We need to stop walking." Olga raised her voice. "Peter, when are we going to …" The words died in her mouth. The miles of darkness ahead of them had now taken form as if the shadows had risen from the ground. A silhouette at least one hundred feet tall dominated the horizon. A wall of black.

"Is that the wall?" Matilda said.

Peter halted and spun around. She'd not spoken any louder than they had for most of their conversation. If he'd heard that …

"The wall?" Peter said, and then shook his head. "I wouldn't call it *the* wall, just a wall." He looked past the girls and raised a hand in Carl's direction, instructing him to halt. Keep his distance and there wouldn't be any trouble. It seemed like a well-rehearsed routine. How many times had he had to restrain Carl in the past? How many times had he failed?

Despite him swaying where he stood, muttering to himself the entire time, Carl followed his friend's commands. Olga shrugged. "*A* wall, *the* wall, what's the difference?"

"They're worlds apart, my dear. This is the funnel, a way to separate the north and the south. Only experienced travellers can pass through here, but if you know the way, which we do, then it's perfectly safe. *The* wall, however, is a place of insanity. Very few have visited it and lived to tell the tale. They say to touch it is to open the door to madness. As far as I know, no one has crossed it."

"It's worth crossing?"

Peter shrugged. "Who knows? But they say there's a better life on the other side."

"Of the few who have gotten close enough to touch it and return, all of them have paid the price."

Matilda gasped when Peter looked at Carl. She said, "*He's* been?"

"As close as anyone I know, but don't you *ever* talk to him about it." Peter pointed at a building no more than one hundred feet away. A tower in a better state of repair than the rest of their surroundings. "This is our destination. This is where we'll rest tonight. In the morning, we shall pass through the funnel, and then we have one more day's travel to get to Grandfather Jacks. We'll get there with plenty of time."

"For what?" Olga said.

"Come on."

"I said for what? What sick plan do you have for us?"

From the way Matilda walked, stumbling on what must have been tired legs, she needed the rest. And Olga couldn't fight for the both of them.

A tower Peter must have climbed before, because the route to the next level didn't present itself. The retired hunter showed Matilda the way by tapping the first step with his foot.

With Peter's help, Matilda scrambled up to the first floor. When he pushed her bottom to help her all the way up, Olga snarled, "If you touch my arse like that, I'll kick your fucking teeth out."

Peter smiled and helped Olga like he had Matilda, keeping her steady by holding her bonds instead of her bottom.

Olga breathed deeply against the pain in her shoulder blades and wobbled at the final part of the climb as the thought of falling flipped through her. Joining Matilda in the far corner of the first floor, Olga dropped to her knees, slamming down on the hard stone, her legs tired, her hands still bound. Turning her back to the wall, she fell against it.

"Carl will keep guard on the ground," Peter said, smiling as he closed in on the girls.

As the man drew closer, a writhe turned through Olga. The muscles in her right leg twitched with a need to lash out. To keep him at bay.

But Peter sat down cross-legged several feet away. The shadows hid most of his features other than the slight shimmer in his dark feline eyes, and the glint of his teeth when he smiled. "I just wanted to say a prayer to Grandfather Jacks before we sleep for the night."

Her jaw still clamped tight, Olga inhaled through her nose.

While bowing his head, Peter addressed the floor, "Thank you, Grandfather Jacks, for allowing us safe passage through the wasteland today. For keeping us from harm until we got to our checkpoint. Thank you for blessing myself and Carl with the chance to deliver these two virgin souls into your care. These two lost sheep, who will receive your guidance on their path to enlightenment. We are so lucky to be a part of that, and we will do all you require of us because you have shown us what it means to serve you. It's our honour for now and for evermore. Praise be to the High Father."

When Peter looked up, Olga remained frozen still, her jaw loose.

A storm cloud settled on his features, a livid vein lifting a line along his left temple before he barked, "Give thanks!"

"Thank you, Grandfather Jacks," Matilda said.

Where would it get them for Olga to tell him to go screw himself and Grandfather Jacks? Matilda was right, she needed to pick her battles. Another deep breath, she filled her lungs, her chest rising before she dipped a nod. "Thank you, Grandfather Jacks." Would they have been safer with Carl in the building with them instead of Peter?

As the engorged vein on Peter's forehead settled, his smile broadened and his eyes regained their feline grace. He shifted close to Olga so just a few inches separated them. Glistening tear tracks streaked his cheeks. He stroked the left side of her face with a trembling hand. "Thank you. You two are in for such a treat when you meet the High Father."

Several waves of revulsion rippled away from Peter's touch. Olga stared at the moon, fighting against her quickening pulse. At least Carl wore his insanity on his sleeve. Peter seemed like he had crazy in his core. At what point would it spill over?

CHAPTER 6

The voices penetrated William's dreams and he opened his eyes. Several blinks did little to clear the bleary lens through which he viewed the world. Where he went to bed shivering, he woke up the same way, his clothes still damp, the hard and cold brick wall offering support but little comfort. Every muscle in his body had locked tight, frozen solid because of the harsh conditions. Thank god they hadn't been dragged into following the girls in the middle of winter.

Artan and Max stood by the window on the building's first floor, chatting to one another. The grainy light of the early morning around them, mist hung in the air, and condensation billowed from their mouths.

William battled his trembling body and pushed himself to his feet before stumbling over to his friends. They were both focused on something outside the building. When he got closer to the window, he said, "What the hell is that?"

A large wall dominated the horizon, stretching across the landscape as far as William could see. Tens of feet tall, black and gnarly. As imposing as a mountain range, but too straight along the top to have been formed by nature.

William pulled the map from his back pocket. Considerably more wrinkled and damp than the last time he'd looked at it. Max bent down, retrieved something from the floor, and handed it to him.

Clear plastic. William held it for a second.

"To cover the map," Max said. "Otherwise it will turn to mush, and then how will we find Grandfather Jacks' community?"

While wrapping the unfolded map, William said, "Is this the wall the woman you were in prison with spoke of?"

Max fixed on the map with a deep frown. Since they'd left Umbriel, Max fixed on everything with a deep frown. "Aren't we too far north for that?" The thick line dissecting the depicted land sat much lower down the map than their current spot. Max pointed at the much thinner line north of it. "This could be what we're looking at. Like the main wall, it looks like it runs coast to coast."

"*The* wall, *a* wall. I suppose it doesn't matter," William said. "The fact is, we need to get past it if we're to get to Grandfather Jacks' community."

While scratching his closely cropped brown hair, Artan said, "And before we even try, we need to find Cyrus."

Cyrus was dead. They all knew that, and the loss of the boy weighed heavy, but Artan clearly hadn't accepted it. And how long would that take? The question sat on the tip of William's tongue, but he chewed it back. Instead, he turned to Max. "Are you okay?"

The stoic boy nodded. "I'm fine, why?"

"You've not said much since we left Umbriel."

"I'm not sure there's much to say."

Artan barged past William on his way to the edge of the first floor. "Come on, we let you sleep because we figured you needed the rest, but now we need to look for Cyrus."

Max raised his eyebrows and William nodded. Artan wouldn't take no for an answer regardless of what either of them thought. They needed to find the boy, or at least make the gesture of trying to find him. The sooner Artan gave up on him, the sooner they could move on.

William's already cold and damp trousers picked up the early morning dew from the long grass. His clothes clung tighter to him than before, but at least it had stopped raining. They'd entered the town in the darkness. The silhouettes had shown the number of buildings surrounding them, but the details had been hidden. At least fifty structures of varying sizes, moss covered a lot of the brickwork. How much longer before nature reclaimed this small town? "You want us to search them all, Artan?"

Matilda's brother led them back to where they'd been fighting the previous evening. "If that's what it takes."

Max must have been thinking it too, so William shrugged. Someone needed to say it. "At what point do we give up?"

"When we've searched every inch of this ruined town."

Every answer came back like the crack of a whip. A hard snap to his words, but they needed to have the conversation, and because Max hadn't said much since Umbriel, the responsibility had fallen to William. "Maybe he's been bitten and moved on?"

"Do you even care he's gone?"

"*I* was the one who wanted to save him, remember? We owed him for his help in the national service area."

"But what about now? You owe him more now than ever. He'd still be with us if you'd stopped when everyone else wanted to."

"Well, screw me for wanting to make sure your sister and Olga are okay."

"At this rate, you'll be the only one making it to them. We

need to look after ourselves so we can be of some use when we find them."

Although William drew a breath to reply, Artan cut him off, reaching the first of the slain bodies they'd left from their fight the previous evening. "Anyway, if he's turned, he'll be here. When have you ever known a diseased to get infected and then run away from people?"

If William had a reply, he would have given it.

"Exactly," Artan said.

As Max turned over a diseased woman, shorter than Cyrus, with long blonde hair and pale skin, he said, "This feels like when I was looking for my family in Edin."

"You found them all, right?" Artan said.

"That's supposed to be a consolation?"

"No. But it suggests when they turned, they didn't go far. Which is why I don't want to give up looking for Cyrus until we know what's happened to him for certain."

At least flipping dead bodies drove the cold from William's bones. His breathing grew heavier; his brow dampened with sweat. His dirty skin itched beneath his sodden clothes.

As Artan turned over the final body—a large man with a deep gash across his face—William twisted Jezebel's shaft, spinning the double-headed axe.

Flushed from the workout, Artan had his war hammer slung over one shoulder. He ran a hand over his head, his cheeks puffing out when he exhaled. He spun on the spot, avoiding eye contact with William before he handed Max his weapon and ran towards the building closest to them. One of the taller structures, the old church had lost its spire, but its first floor remained intact. While grunting, Artan pulled himself up into the old loft.

Despite the distance between him and Artan, William still

spoke to Max from the side of his mouth so as not to be heard. "This feels like a lost cause, right?"

"We have to try though. I'd want you to try if you were looking for me. Cyrus is one of us now."

"Diseased!" Artan called down, pointing away from him. "Just one of them."

The slightest change in Max's expression. A hint of excitement broke through his stern fix, and his eyes widened. He raised the war hammer and said, "I've got this."

The church and a row of four terrace houses beside it blocked William's view of the diseased. An alleyway ran between them, the grass only two to three feet tall from where the road had once been paved. The swishing of a stumbling form headed their way. The tight alley caught its slathering breaths, but William still couldn't see it.

Max stepped closer to the opening and William raised Jezebel. Artan continued his search from the church's roof.

The creature burst from the alleyway. An explosion of limbs and yelling fury, it slashed at the air. What few teeth it had, it displayed, its cracked and bloody lips pulled back in a snarl, a blackened wound revealing a hole in its cheek. Max might have been closer, but it fixed its crimson stare on William. Its next scream died before it could release it from its filled lungs, Max slamming the war hammer over the top of the creature's head.

The wet crack snapped William's stomach tense, and the back of his knees tingled as if his legs might fail him. It didn't matter how many diseased they'd killed, his senses were yet to dull to the acts of extreme violence. Especially in the cold light of day.

The absence of Max's smile up until that point only hit home now he beamed at his accomplishment. While staring at the hammer, turning it over in his grip, he laughed. "I need to get myself one of these."

"Look!" Artan remained on the church's roof, now pointing down into the alley the diseased had just burst from. Instead of explaining further, he took off across the church's first floor, leaped a low wall that must have once separated rooms, and jumped through the open wall at the end to the ground at least ten feet below.

William followed Max into the alley and called to Artan, "You sure there weren't any more diseased?"

"I couldn't see any."

"So what are we looking at?" Max said.

Artan pointing down explained nothing. The boy then dropped into a crouch and traced the lines with his finger to better show them. A large metal disc embedded in the ground, it had moss surrounding it. Several lines of fresh scrapes had been torn through the green vegetation. "This cover has been moved recently."

The disc stretched about a foot and a half in diameter. It mostly covered a hole, a small gap along its side from where it hadn't been properly replaced. Artan wedged his fingers into the space and William stepped back. "You don't know what's down there. What if you get bitten?"

If Artan heard him, he ignored him, dragging the heavy metal disc aside, the steel scraping over the concrete as he revealed a deep and dark hole.

"You're not going down there, are you?" William said.

"I'm not giving up on him."

"But what if that hole's filled with diseased?"

"*You* wanted to run through the night to get to Matilda and Olga. You wanted to run blind, and that's why Cyrus got separated from us, so please don't start trying to be cautious now."

"Let me go down there," Max said. "It makes sense."

Artan hesitated at the hole's entrance. "You sure?"

"No, but it makes sense."

The second Max lowered his leg into the hole, the dark pit squeaked.

"Cyrus?" Artan said, his call echoing in the hole.

All three boys waited for a second until the febrile voice responded, "Yes. It's me."

"Cyrus?" Artan leaned into the hole when Max stepped aside. "What are you doing down there?"

Ladder rungs ran all the way down the side wall. They'd been there all along, but it had taken for Artan to start climbing for William to notice them. The space looked similar to the one they'd used to climb from the tunnel near Magma's community. What use had the underground paths had in the old world?

Cyrus emerged from the darkness.

Artan helped him out by holding a hand down to him. He hugged the boy when he'd pulled him free of the hole.

William shoved Cyrus and Artan aside with his left arm and brought Jezebel over in a wide arc. Not built to be used with one hand, William lacked the accuracy required to end the female diseased, burying the large axe head in the beast's shoulder. It opened a deep red wound, unsettled the creature's balance, and threw her and Jezebel into the right wall of the alley before she fell to the ground, screaming and kicking her legs.

Max crushed her head with one swing of Artan's war hammer.

The boys paused, waiting for more, but only the wind called through the buildings.

"What were you doing down there?" Artan said, hugging Cyrus again. "Why didn't you come back up?"

Glazed eyes, a tear ran down Cyrus' dark cheek. "Because I ran away like a coward. I got surrounded by diseased and I ran."

"And why wouldn't you?"

"Because no one else did."

"Max doesn't need to run away, and William and I can fight the diseased. We've had plenty of practice."

"But what good am I to the group if I run at the first sign of trouble? I'm slow and I can't fight. I'm a liability."

Cyrus trembled beneath William's comforting hand. He squeezed his shoulder and waited for the boy to make eye contact. His deep brown eyes fixed on William before dropping to the ground again. "You did the right thing," William said. "You kept yourself safe. If you don't feel confident fighting, at least you looked after yourself. We all have something to bring to the group."

A shake of his head, Cyrus said, "I don't."

"We got into trouble last night because of me, and for that I'm sorry."

"You're not mad at me?" Cyrus said.

"Of course not."

"Have you had any sleep?" Artan said.

Cyrus shook his head.

The words stuck in William's throat and it took a second to get them out. "Do you need to get some now? We can stand guard while you take a nap."

Cyrus shook his head again. "We need to get moving. The longer we wait, the farther we'll fall behind the girls."

"Thank you," William said. "Are you sure you're ready to move on?"

"I'm sure." Cyrus pointed at the dark wall on the horizon. "What's that?"

"We don't know." Max handed the war hammer back to

Artan, holding onto it for a little longer than he needed to. "But we're about to find out."

CHAPTER 7

They'd been walking through the funnel since first light several hours previously. A cold spring morning, it had been misty when they woke, and that mist remained. Olga's nose and ears stung from where the sensation returned to them after being numb all night. Her bound wrists burned, the damp rope eating away at her skin.

The hunters had often returned to Edin with salvaged steel, so Olga had seen it before, but only ever in small quantities. She couldn't have imagined the miles of it now beneath her feet and stretching beyond her vision in either direction. The entire wall had been constructed purely from the cold grey metal. They walked through the lowest part, a deep crevice they called the funnel. At its lowest point, the funnel still stood about seventy feet from the ground. The deep gorge condensed the bitter wind into an icy blast. Olga walked with a hunch, dipping her head against the blustery assault.

The surface was uneven, rocklike in its formation. Olga's foot slipped again on the dew-coated surface, her pulse spiking at the potential bone-breaking fall. Keeping up with

Peter's pace forced large white clouds of condensation from her. She might have asked him to slow down, but since the weirdness of the previous evening, she'd only spoken to him when absolutely necessary.

Not that it stopped Peter talking to them, the smaller man either oblivious to how he'd made them feel, or he simply didn't care. "So, as I was saying, girls, the funnel is the only way through this wall. The wall itself stretches from coast to coast, and this is the only path. Every other part is too sheer to climb."

"Why is it here?" Olga said. She might as well talk to him. They were going to have to spend time with them both anyway.

"Who built it, you mean?"

Like he had towards the end of the previous day, Carl continued to follow them at a safe distance. Over forty feet behind, he checked over his shoulder many times and chatted to himself as if trying to appease the demons he carried with him.

"Yeah," Olga said. She checked on Carl again when he raised his voice and spun one way and then the other, watching the sky as if the voices he'd been speaking to had taken form and came at him in a winged assault.

"It was built to stop the troubles from the south of the wall spreading north."

"It's that bad in the south?" Matilda said. If she struggled with the walk, it didn't show. Looser than she'd been from Carl's beating, she now hopped from one high point to another like a cat along the top of a fence.

Peter smiled, his feline eyes narrowing. "To some it is, but you know what fear does to people. They think building walls and killing others is a way to manage their own insecurities. They blame everyone else for their fragility. I think the south's wonderful. And this wall's worked in our favour. The only people who can pass through here with any kind of certainty are those blessed by Grandfather Jacks. The prophet lights the way."

The most challenging part of their journey so far—other than the company of the two men—had been trying to match Peter's pace. What did he mean about the prophet lighting the way?

Clearly buzzing with being their guide, Peter ran with a hop, skip, and jump to one of the higher spots. He shielded his brow against the rising sun. "We're nearly there." He then spun, pointed at Olga's foot and shouted, "Stop!"

It had been all but invisible until Peter had brought it to her attention. A square foot of metal in Olga's path, the outline of it too faint to be obvious. A small panel. A trigger of some sort. "What is it?"

Peter leaped to another high spot on the funnel and peered down on something Olga couldn't see. A sadistic grin spread across his slim face.

Matilda passed Olga and gasped when she joined Peter. Olga caught up a few seconds later, her legs burning from climbing without the use of her hands. The new angle revealed what stepping on the trigger would have done. The path in front of them would have fallen away. It would have thrown them into a chute with a dogleg bend in it that ended in a pit about six feet square, the sheer walls at least ten feet tall. The entire trap made from the same cold dark steel, the pit had a carpet of spikes lining the bottom. Each spike stood about two feet tall. If they didn't kill the victim instantly, they would do enough damage to cause a slow and painful death. Had Peter halted Olga a second later … She shook her head to banish the thought.

"Well, well," Peter said, "what have we here, then?"

The pit and spikes had taken all of Olga's attention. She hadn't even seen the hands clinging on to the end of the chute.

It made Olga's skin crawl to move closer to Peter, but it gave her a clear view of the woman with her brown hair clinging to her sweating face. Her mouth stretched with the agony of clinging on, her eyebrows pinched in the middle. She grunted against the effort it took to speak. "Please help me. I don't know how much longer I can stay here."

While resting his hands on his hips, his two spears in their holder on his back, his long knife at his belt, Peter threw his head back, forced his stomach forwards, and laughed at the clouds.

The woman's already wide blue eyes widened. "Please," she said to Olga and Matilda, "do something."

Olga turned her back on the woman to show her the bonds.

"You know what this is?" Peter said.

The woman looked back to him, her face chalky white.

"This is a test of faith."

"A test of what faith?"

Peter laughed again and Olga distanced herself from the man, his shrill cackle turning her blood cold. "Don't tell me you don't have *any* faith?"

"I have faith in strangers."

"Nice try."

"Then what the hell are you talking about?"

"So you believe in hell? That's something, I suppose. Do you follow Grandfather Jacks?"

"Who?"

Peter ran along the side of the chute and stopped close to the woman. Close enough to reach down and pull her out. The handle of the knife on his belt poked away from his body when he crouched. Olga's hands twitched with the need to grab it. "My dear, you have much to learn. I'm going to teach you about faith, and it might just save your life."

"Why don't you just pull me out? That would save my life."

"What will that teach you? Now, the person who has faith would let go."

Tears shimmered in the woman's glare. "Why would I do that?"

"Just help her, Peter," Matilda said.

Peter spun around, his soft face hardening. "Do you want to join her?" After a pause, he turned back to the woman, his voice calm again. "Now, where were we? Faith, that's it. The person with faith would let go now."

Olga's hand twitched again as she watched the wooden knife handle, electric pain streaking away from the cuts on her wrists.

"But there's a pit of spikes down there," the woman said.

"Or is that all you see? When you need guidance in the darkness, your mind might tell you there are monsters ahead. But if you take the hand of the High Father and believe in what he can do for you, then you'll be all right." All trace of the malice he'd flashed at Matilda now gone, a wide smile filled his face, his dark eyes pinching at the sides. "We could all do with a little more faith. Just trust me, sweetheart, you'll be okay."

The woman trembled worse than before and shook her head.

"It's the only way to freedom," Peter said. "Trust me, I know the funnel as well as anyone."

The woman frowned and fought to get her words out through stuttering breaths. "You're sure?"

"Absolutely. This is just a test, my dear."

Olga winced when the woman let go and screamed as she dropped. She fell into the pit, her cry dying in her throat. If someone had asked Olga why she'd stepped forward at that moment, she wouldn't have been able to answer. For some reason, she needed to see if the woman had made it. But of course she hadn't. Peter hadn't come here to save her. Skewered on several spikes, the glistening and bloody tip of one protruded from her open mouth.

His hands raised in prayer, Peter closed his eyes and faced the sky. "Praise be to Grandfather Jacks. May you help this lost soul on her journey to redemption in the afterlife. May you watch over her until she sees the error of her ways. Hell is a place where the unenlightened dwell. Let us pray she learns never to use that word again."

Carl fizzed and hissed, Olga screaming in response to the outburst. But he aimed his rage at Peter. His teeth bared, his eyes wild, he sneered at his partner.

If Peter knew he'd become the focus of Carl's rage, he hid it well. If the woman's death had meant anything to him, it didn't show. He spoke like a tour guide taking the girls on a little jaunt. "So you've now seen what some of the traps are like in the funnel. Some of them are so old they don't go off, but it's hard to predict, so assume all of them will work. Just follow my lead and you'll be fine. Anyone guided by Grandfather Jacks can find their way through here. Anyway, let's move on, shall we? It won't be long before we're off the funnel and that one step closer to the High Father."

Olga raised her eyebrows at Matilda. At what point should they fight back? How long before it got too late to act?

"Grandfather Jacks, my arse," Carl said. Heavy bags sat beneath his eyes, his ruddy cheeks hanging, a white band underlining each iris. His stare remained glazed and lacked focus. "There's no salvation with him. If hell exists anywhere, it's where that man resides."

However they did it, Olga and Matilda needed to find a way out of this mess before they were delivered to the High Father.

~

They'd walked for several more hours, the day growing long. Peter had pointed out many of the trips and triggers along their way. "And we have another one," he said a few hours later. "As the prophet sent his men to lead the pure through the treacherous path, they encountered many obstacles. They found the devil's outstretched hand in various forms. Those who took it were lured into darkness."

"What the hell?" Carl spat, twisting as if possessed. His head snapped one way and then the other. He rocked back and forth. "The prophet! Ha! The devil more like. Cleanse them of their sins! As if the prophet doesn't commit heinous acts. Sins. What does that even mean?" The words fell from his mouth as if he couldn't contain them, and he banged the palm of his hand against his wide forehead. Just speaking them seemed to cause him physical pain.

This time, a man had been caught in a trap. A pit similar to the one the woman had fallen into, except there were no spikes. Short and in his mid thirties, the man had a bald spot on the top of his head. He paced back and forth in his prison.

When Peter crouched down on the edge of the hole, his knife protruded from his belt again. The spears remained in his sheath on his back. He had no worries, and why should he? The man in the pit couldn't do anything, Carl seemed like more of a danger to himself, and Matilda and Olga were bound so tight he had total control over them.

Another twitch snapped through Olga's right hand, and she gripped the air as she imagined holding the knife's wooden handle. If she charged him, he might drop the knife. It might give them an opening.

Matilda shook her head. She'd clearly read Olga's thoughts.

"Confess your sins!" Peter said to the man.

The man scrunched his face, squinting as he looked up into the sun. "What are you talking about?"

"Confess your sins," Peter said.

"*What* sins?"

"You tell me. Salvation only comes from the pure of spirit. The free of heart. Let me help you relinquish your sins. I can ease your burden, brother."

The man's face twisted and his eyes glazed. At first he looked like he might tell Peter where to go. But his expression buckled. "I ran away from her. She needed me and I ran. I left her hanging over the pit of spikes when I heard you coming. Is she okay? Did you save her?"

While hooking a thumb over his shoulder, Peter smiled, his voice so soft the strong wind nearly overpowered him. "She's back there. She's saved now."

"Thank god."

Peter's features hardened. "What god?"

"Huh?"

"What god do you speak of? Who do you thank?"

"W-w-what does it matter?"

The crouched Peter formed an imposing silhouette as he hunched on the edge of the pit. "*What does it matter?* It might not matter to you. If it did, you wouldn't be in this situation."

A panel to trigger another trap. Similar to the one Olga nearly stood on that led to the spiked pit. It remained slightly depressed. The man must have activated it, but it hadn't reset.

Peter tapped it with his toe. Once. Twice. He grinned and leaned on it. *Click!*

The thunderous rumble of an avalanche shook the steel beneath Olga's feet. Boulders and rocks spilled from a hole high up, a slope leading from them to the pit containing the man. They raced towards him, some of them two to three feet in diameter.

The man's scream ended in a *crunch!* Nailed by the first rock.

Serenity spread across Peter's face and he nodded at the girls. "And that's why you're better with us. We're on the winning team. You'd do well to learn that. There is only one god, and you are among the lucky few who will be welcomed into the warm embrace of his love. Isn't that right, Carl?"

Carl's mouth spread wide in a battle cry and he charged at Peter. His feet twisted and turned with the uneven surface, but he moved along the funnel as if it were flat. On the run, he drew one of his spears and threw it.

"What's gotten into you, man?" Peter called out as he ducked the projectile.

Carl flashed past the girls and Olga's stomach lurched. He'd been inches from knocking her down.

"Fuck Grandfather Jacks. He's the devil." When Carl slammed into Peter, both of them hit the steel hard. The skittering sound of metal against metal, Carl's knife broke from his hip and spun away from the scuffling pair. The wooden handle dared Olga to grab it.

"What the fuck do you know about the salvation Grandfather Jacks offers?" Carl grabbed Peter by the lapels, dominating the smaller man as he loomed over him. He headbutted him, hitting his nose with a thunder crack. "You talk about sin like he does. Like you're an authority when you're nothing but a hypocrite."

As Peter reached up, wrapping a strong grip around Carl's neck, Olga nudged Matilda and nodded at Carl's knife. No more than ten feet from where they stood, the blade at least eight inches long. Long enough to take the fight to the men if they could get free of their bonds.

Matilda raised her eyebrows and pulled her hands away from her back. "How can we do anything?"

"We could use it to cut ourselves free."

Matilda shook her head. "We won't be able to move quickly enough."

The men grunted and yelled as they wrestled one another, oblivious to Olga and Matilda's conversation.

"Come on, you've had a rest now," Olga said. "Let's do this. We wait any longer and we'll miss our opportunity."

Matilda shook her head again.

"Screw this!" Olga took off in the direction of the knife. By her third step, Matilda chased after her.

CHAPTER 8

The map remained in the plastic sleeve Max had found, William referencing it again before he said, "This wall looks like it stretches as wide as the entire map." The closer they got to the large black barrier, the taller it seemed to grow. "I've never seen so much steel in my life." The gunmetal grey face of it stood sheer. It might have been covered in scratches and scars, but in comparison to the crumbling world around them, this barrier remained strong and resolute. About one hundred feet tall, it had just one path running through it as a deep crevice.

Cyrus shivered, the day yet to warm up. "How long do you reckon it'll take to cross?"

"God knows," Artan said. "We don't know how deep it is. What do you think, Max?"

Again, the boy had very few words. Artan's spear raised and ready to use, he simply shrugged.

His war hammer in a two-handed grip, Artan held it towards Max. "Are you pissed that I won't give you this?"

"No."

"Well, what is it, then?" William said. "You've been miserable for days."

"I don't know if you've noticed, but we're not exactly living an idyllic existence right now."

"Sure, but it takes some serious effort to be as moody as you've been for as long as you have."

His voice warbling with his shivering form, Cyrus said, "It's about what happened with you and Olga, isn't it?"

Of course William knew what had gotten him down, but they needed to get it out in the open. And maybe he should have been more sympathetic, but when Max's lips tightened and his frown deepened, he said, "What did you expect? You publicly humiliated her."

Max turned, his spear raised. "I didn't expect her to kiss Hawk!"

While wringing his axe handle, William widened his stance. He spoke through clenched teeth. "Maybe if you'd talked to her beforehand, none of this would have happened."

"Maybe if you'd taken us away from Umbriel rather than deciding we'd be okay going on one hunt—"

Artan dropped his hammer and caught William, dragging him back before he could charge at Max.

Max remained rooted to the spot. Cold blue eyes, he'd fight William if he wanted it, and he didn't care if he lost. "Why are you suddenly on Olga's side anyway?"

After he'd shaken Artan off, Matilda's brother remaining between him and Max, William straightened his still-damp clothes. "I'm on the side of reason."

"Shame you weren't on the side of reason last night when you nearly got us all killed."

"They can't kill *you*."

"But unlike you, I care about the group's safety."

As Artan guided William farther away, Cyrus walked

over to Max and said, "I think we could all learn to communicate better and think about others more, wouldn't you say? And I think the point William's trying to make is that Olga needed to know how you felt. It seems like all the drama between you both could have been avoided had she been able to make an informed choice about your relationship."

The boy's softness might have made him a liability in a fight, but Cyrus' smooth tone moved through the group like hot steam. The muscles in William's back relaxed.

Even Max let go of a lot of the rigidity in his frame. He nodded several times as if psyching himself up to get his words out. "Cyrus is right. I didn't explain myself very well. I think Olga would have behaved very differently had she known. I fear we won't find them again and I'll never get to explain. I wonder where they are now. Do they even know we're still alive? That we're trying to get to them?"

"Until we know otherwise," Cyrus said, "we have to assume they're okay. With nothing to cling onto, we might as well reach for hope."

His legs aching from all the travelling they'd done and the promise of much more to come, William's feet slammed down as he fell from one step into another. He let go of a hard sigh. They'd reach the wall in the next ten minutes, and then they'd have to climb it. "So what do you reckon? We go through the path in the wall? I'm guessing it's the quickest route."

"It makes me uneasy that the path has already been chosen for us," Artan said.

A gap in the clouds burned William's eyes as the sun found its way through.

Max raised a hand to his brow to help see better. "But what other choice do we have? I don't know about you boys, but I'm not sure I could climb any other part of it."

"We could look for another way around?" Cyrus said.

"William," Max said, "does the map show the path?"

William unfolded the map again. Two parallel diagonal lines ran across the wall. They were close together and were in the same spot as the path. "I think so."

Cyrus said, "And are there any others?"

"I don't think so."

"The map's been reliable so far," Max said. "I say we use the path."

William nodded. "If the girls have come this way, I reckon they crossed here."

"And what we know," Max added, "is there's a path in front of us right now. Who knows how long it will take to find another one. If there even is another one."

While shaking his head, Cyrus said, "I don't like it."

"I'm not sure any of us do, but let's take a vote," Max said. "I'm up for using the path."

"I don't think I am," Cyrus said. "Sorry."

"I'll take it," William said.

"I don't like it either," Artan said.

William leaned closer to Matilda's brother. "What other—"

"But," Artan cut him off, "I don't think we'll find any better options than this. I say we cross it."

∼

SWEAT RAN INTO WILLIAM'S EYES AND HE STRETCHED HIS mouth wide to fill his lungs as he managed the sharp incline. He led the way up the cold steel path. "Imagine if we'd tried to go up any other part of this wall."

The others followed him in single file, Artan at the back, helping Cyrus manage the climb.

They said little until they reached the path, William holding a hand down to Artan to help him with the final few steps. The ground uneven like rock, the crevice funnelled the wind, William clamping his jaw against the biting cold.

Cyrus walked ahead as Artan stood straight, the sunshine glistening off his sweating face. He placed his hands on his hips and said, "Looks like we have a long way to go."

Click!

Cyrus stopped and spun around. His face had fallen slack. He stood on a section of the ground no more than a foot square. It had depressed beneath his weight.

"What—" The wall on William's left and Cyrus' right fell away, cutting William's words off, the ground tilting towards the hole that had opened.

All four of them slipped, a sharp nauseating sting crashing through William's left hip when he hit the side wall on his way down the chute.

The wide funnel narrowed, dragging in Artan, William, Max behind him, and then Cyrus at the back. The chute spat them into a pit one after the other. Artan fell first, the effect of the twenty-foot drop lessened by his slamming into the opposite wall before he hit the ground. If William could have landed anywhere but on his friend, he would have, holding his battle-axe above his head so he didn't cleave the boy in two. He then threw it away from him moments before white light punched through his vision when Max landed, kicking him in the side of the face as he added to the crumpled heap. The air left his lungs when Cyrus fell on top of them all.

The space just wide enough for all four of them, the walls sheer, they all groaned and complained as they stood up. The chute, twenty feet above them, was the closest way out. The top of the pit stood at least ten feet higher. "What the hell is this place?" William said.

"What's that?" Cyrus pointed up. A cage sat at the top of the pit. A wire mesh bucket the size of at least three bathtubs, it had been filled with shards of glass. Some of the pieces were large enough to cut someone in two. It sat on the edge of its balance.

"Is that thing supposed to tip on us?" Max said.

As if responding to his words, the cage teetered for a second before it fell towards them.

Cyrus screamed.

Artan yelled.

William covered his head with his hands.

CHAPTER 9

Olga dropped to one knee on the hard steel. The shock of the contact sent a spasm up the front of her thigh that culminated in a tight clench in her groin. While biting down hard, she turned around and grabbed Carl's wayward knife, feeling for it with her hands. On her first attempt, she batted the handle, sending the long blade spinning. It nicked her finger with a sharp sting, but it halted the blade's rotation.

The two men continued fighting. Peter mounted Carl. He might have been the smaller of the two, but the slippery rat moved as if oiled up. He punched down, slamming his fist into Carl's fat nose. His cat's eyes glazed with rage as he fixed on Olga before he punched down again. She'd be next.

Olga found the long blade's handle and pulled it into her bound grip. Her legs shook with the effort of standing without the use of her hands.

Any plans Peter had of following them got derailed when Carl swung for him. His large fist connected with Peter's left ear, knocking him from his perch, slamming him into the hard steel. Carl rolled with him, clambered on top, and pinned him.

"You ready?" Olga said, holding the knife behind her like a tail. The slightest flicker of doubt shimmered across Matilda's face. Give her too much time to think and she'd stay. Olga took off. They wouldn't get a better chance than this.

Olga moved like a flightless bird, the uneven surface threatening to trip her every step. If she went down, she'd end up chewing the hard steel and probably lose her teeth in the process. She shook the thought away. They had to get free from Carl and Peter.

Matilda yelled. Olga halted and turned as her friend lived out her fear. She tripped, twisted in mid-air, and hit the hard steel shoulder first. She skidded, heading straight for—

"Oh, shit!" A trigger like the one that set off the trap with the girl in. A square in the ground, the thin line almost impossible to see. Somehow Olga had missed it. Matilda headed straight for it.

While turning the blade so the tip pointed to the back of her head, Olga charged at her friend, running up the steep side of the funnel on her right. She aimed for Matilda with a two-footed slide, and hit her in the back, changing both of their courses so they missed the button, halting as they collided with the other steep side of the funnel.

Gasping for breath, her face puce, Matilda kicked Olga away from her. "What the hell?"

Having managed to remain on her side the entire time, Olga rolled over onto her front so she didn't stab herself with the knife. She lifted her bottom in the air and brought her knees into her chest before she stood up, teetering on the edge of her balance.

On her feet too, Matilda said, "Well?"

"See that there?" Olga flicked her head in the direction of the button.

Matilda's red face lost its colour, her tanned skin turning sheet white. "Another trap?"

Olga shrugged.

"T-thank you."

"You fall, I fall. We're in this together, okay?"

Matilda nodded.

The men continued fighting where they'd left them. "Now let's get moving," Olga said. Aching more than before, she led them away again, her hip now bruised and stinging with the graze she'd torn into it.

The funnel took them on a steep incline, which set fire to Olga's leg muscles. She halted at the top, the wind so strong it threatened to throw her back down again. The air left her lungs in a gasp. "Wow!" She shook her head as Matilda joined her.

"What is this place?" Matilda said.

"South of the wall," Olga said.

Matilda fought for breath. "South of *a* wall."

Similar meadows to those in the north stretched away from them. The landscape barren like many spots they'd seen before. But on this side, giant rocks of steel were scattered through the grass. Failed projects, or maybe excess material used for building the wall. Like the ruins in the north, nature took a slow and inevitable possession of the scenery, moss and rust growing on the large chunks. They were much more resilient than the buildings in the north.

The sun found a gap in the clouds, lighting up the path before them. The funnel showed the way off this wall, the path dropping to the ground at a hazardous gradient.

"I'm inclined to turn back to see if we can find the boys."

"Me too," Olga said. "But—"

"Carl and Peter."

"Right. We need to lose them first. Here, let me cut you

—" A roar from behind. Peter had broken free and had reached the bottom of the incline. He stared up at the two girls. Olga froze.

Carl appeared a second later, tackling Peter to the ground, slamming down on top of him.

"Follow me." Olga took off down the slope towards the meadow, her heart in her throat, her legs moving faster than she could control.

The slam of Matilda's feet behind her, she panted for breath. "We need to find somewhere to hide."

Olga gripped the knife at her back, the buzz of rope burns wrapping her wrists. Unable to control her speed, she watched her steps, a millisecond to pick each one before she committed.

Matilda tripped again, hit the ground with an, "Ooomph," slid along the steel, and cleaned out Olga's legs.

Olga spun in mid-air to keep the knife away from her friend. She landed on her front, her chest taking the impact of her fall. A nauseating clench gripped her stomach. As she yelled, she lost her grip on Carl's knife, the weapon sliding with the two girls, all three of them racing down the rough chute.

The knife flew farther than Olga, embedding in the ground tip first. The soft meadow cushioned her fall, but Matilda clattered into her for a second time.

A shrill cry snapped Olga rigid and drove the pain from her body. The ground damp beneath her turned her trousers sodden when she got up onto one knee to stand. She turned to retrieve the knife. For what good it would do. Not much use if she couldn't get her hands free.

Men and women, six of them. They lacked the atrophied limbs and rotting wounds they'd become accustomed to when encountering the diseased in the wild.

"They look like the ones from Edin," Matilda said.

Olga's pulse rocked her body. "Like they've only just turned. But they haven't seen us yet."

"Yet." Matilda bounced on the spot, widened her stance and bent her knees.

"We can't fight them with our hands tied," Olga said. "Turn around."

The creatures no more than twenty feet away, Olga spoke from the side of her mouth, keeping her voice low. "Turn around now." She spun the blade in her grip and pointed the knife out behind her. "Cut your ropes on this."

"But—"

One of the diseased halted. The canted silhouette stood to attention. They'd seen them. "Do it now!" Olga said.

The knife wobbled in Olga's hands as Matilda rubbed her ropes on the blade.

The diseased charged.

Olga gripped the wooden handle tighter.

Ten feet away. Wild limbs. Bleeding eyes. Snapping jaws.

Matilda broke free, took the knife, and spun on the charging diseased. She kicked out first, sending the front runner backwards. She slammed the long blade into the face of the next woman, stumbling back a step from the creature's momentum.

Olga kicked out at the next man and nearly lost her balance. Like a matador avoiding a bull, she jumped aside when he charged her for a second time. Matilda drove the knife into the back of the diseased man's head. The blade burst through his right eye, spraying rancid blood away from his face.

Matilda dropped down and swiped the legs of another woman. Olga ran to the woman, her jaw clenched as she stamped on the back of her head. The snarling, hissing bitch snapped and threw her arms in the air. She looked like an angry octopus, but she couldn't get up because of Olga's repeated attacks.

The diseased's head mashed into a bloody pulp, but the fight hadn't left her. Matilda stabbed her in the side of her head. She'd already taken out all the others. She cut Olga free.

Another scream. The chorus louder than before. "Shall we stay and fight?" Olga said.

Matilda panted and shook her head. "Why risk it? We don't have enough weapons."

"There." Olga pointed at a hole in the side of the sheer wall they'd just left. A cave ten feet from the ground. "Let's go in there."

"And what if Peter and Carl come?"

"We're armed and our hands are free." Close to twenty diseased came into view from behind a large steel rock. "I'd rather take my chances with two old men than that lot."

When they reached the wall, the diseased closing in, Olga boosted Matilda so she could grab the ledge.

Matilda disappeared into the hole, turned around and reached down.

A two-step run-up, Olga kicked off the brushed steel and caught her friend's hands. Matilda dragged her into the safety of their little cave.

The small space no more than ten feet square and dark, it threw the girls' pants back at them as if mocking their exhaustion.

"I'm sorry I made a break for it without consulting you," Olga said.

Matilda swallowed. Olga's throat ached with dehydration too. "It's okay. It was the correct choice. They gave me such a beating the last time, it made me too cautious. Too scared. Thank you for taking the initiative."

"I won't let them beat you like that again. It was my fault you took a kicking."

"You were just trying to save us."

"Still. I'm sorry." While twirling the knife in her hands, Olga said, "the second I see Peter or Carl, I'm going to cut them open."

Matilda smiled and closed her eyes as she leaned her head back against the wall. "I'd like to see that."

CHAPTER 10

But the cage didn't tilt and the glass didn't fall. William remained cowering in the shadow of the bucket of sharp death about to rain down on them. He finally said, "It's stuck."

The others all unfurled, Cyrus' panting on the verge of a panic attack.

"My god," Artan said, "I thought we were done for there."

The brackets along the base of the large basket groaned. Cyrus' scream bounced off the close walls of the cramped pit. "W-w-we might be if we don't get out of here soon."

Max's mood, although dark since they'd left Umbriel, had lightened a little when they were crossing the wall. Wrinkles now dominated his dirt-streaked brow as he turned on Cyrus. "We wouldn't be in this mess if you hadn't triggered the trap."

Artan moved across in front of Cyrus, easing Max back a step. Matilda's brother might have been the youngest, but his wide frame and cardio would be a match for any of them.

"That's not going to help. We should focus on what's going to get us out of here."

Another groan of rusted metal hinges and the basket shifted again. It lurched forward, a large shard about four feet long snapping in half, the top of it spinning as it fell.

Cyrus stood directly in its path. He screamed again and froze. William crashed into the boy, driving the wind from his body as he slammed both of them against the steel wall. The shard dragged a line of wind down his back from where it narrowly missed, smashing as it hit the metal ground.

Max remained fixed on Cyrus, shaking his head and rubbing his shins. His hands came back with blood on them from where the shattering glass had cut him. "That thing isn't going to hold indefinitely. We need a way out. And fast."

But the walls of the pit were as sheer as any William had seen. "The closest exit is that chute." A thin metal bar hung down across the chute's exit, which stood about twenty feet above them. "That bar must have been what triggered the basket to tilt. Maybe we didn't hit it hard enough."

"We hit the wall hard enough," Artan said. "Trust me. And then you lot hit me hard enough."

"I can climb back up the chute," Cyrus said.

Max looked the quivering boy up and down. "When you've finished shitting yourself, you mean?"

"I can do it."

"But how will you get up there?" Artan said.

"If we can stand on each other's shoulders, the biggest at the bottom—"

"Thanks," William said.

"We can make a ladder for me to climb."

"Convenient that it's *you* climbing up and the rest of us staying down here." Max threw his arms up in a shrug. "What if you trigger the trap?"

The tight walls of their pit amplified Cyrus' whining tone. "I can't hold any of you up. Believe me, I *wish* I were stronger."

William said, "It could work. So what will you do when you get up there?"

"I'll get above the basket and empty it. When I've done that, we can tie all our shirts and trousers together and attach them to the cage so you have a way to climb out."

Artan scratched his head. "I can't think of a better plan. And any of us could have triggered that trap."

"But we didn't, did we?"

"Get over it, Max."

While shaking his head, Max took off his shirt and handed it to Cyrus. A moment's pause, he then removed his trousers.

The other boys did the same. They tied their clothes together before wrapping them around Cyrus.

The steel radiated cold, which pressed against William's now semi-naked form. His jaw ached as he clenched it in a futile attempt to control his shivers. As the tallest, William took the lead, widening his stance and pressing his hands against the frigid steel. He dropped his head to allow Artan to climb up his back.

His legs shaking from the weight of Matilda's brother standing on his shoulders, William grunted when Max climbed up him too. The grit on their boot soles and the small particles of glass from the pit's floor cut into his skin.

By the time Max got into place, sweat stood out on William's brow and ran into his eyes. His teeth in a tight clench, he said, "Hurry it up, Cyrus."

Cyrus stepped on William's calf first. It drove a rod of fire through his standing leg. His voice echoed in the pit. "What the hell?" But Cyrus had already climbed him and moved on to Artan.

William let out a hard sigh when Max finally jumped down. Artan hopped off next, and William stood up, stretching the aches from his back and sides.

While wiping the glass dust from his shoulders with light brushes so he didn't tear his hands in the process, William said, "At least he was quick. The only person I know who can climb that fast is …" The word caught on a lump in his throat.

Artan patted William's shoulder. "We will find her, I promise." And then to the frowning Max, "And Olga. We'll find Olga too."

"It's a long way to fall." Cyrus peered down on them from above the cage. Before anyone could tell him to hurry up—William, Max, and Artan standing in their underwear—he got to work. He pinched the next largest shard of glass—a piece about three feet long—and tossed it away from him with the shattering splash of the breaking pane.

The boy moved fast, removing shard after shard, the loud crashes a signal to anyone nearby. And William nearly told him to keep it down. But what did it matter? They needed to get out of there as quickly as possible.

"Yargh!" Cyrus yelled, reaching for the cage, but grabbing air from where it had shifted.

William's stomach turned a backflip. Still half-filled with glass, the large metal basket leaned towards them, the shards shifting inside.

But Cyrus caught it on his second attempt, the momentum of the cage dragging him forwards. He stopped on the edge of his balance. His face locked in a grimace, his eyes wide, he stood on his tiptoes and clung on with his fingertips. He slowly pulled the cage back, the rusted hinges groaning in protest. The cage came farther than before, slamming home with a *splash!*

Max spoke from the side of his mouth. "He could have pulled it towards him in the first place."

"He's doing his best," Artan said.

"I never said he wasn't. That's the problem."

The rest of the large cage now emptied, Cyrus gave the boys a thumbs up. "I'm going to send the rope down."

"Thanks for the commentary," Max said.

The bundle of clothes now in the basket, Cyrus tied one end to the edge before shouting, "Timber!" He pushed the bucket, the large brackets creaking with the movement before the container tipped, slamming down against the sheer steel wall with a sharp *crash!*

A spinning ball of fabric, the clothes unfurled, rolling out as the rope they were intended to be.

"It's too short," Max said, jumping up and missing it by several feet.

"Get on my shoulders." William leaned against the wall for a second time, Max climbing up his back until he stood on him like a ladder. His weight lifted when he caught the bottom of the rope.

"You next," William said to Artan.

"What about you?"

"Let's get you out first. I'll find a way. Or you can find a way for me."

Three of the four of them had made it out and stood around the hole, dressed in only their boxer shorts, socks, and boots. They peered down on William.

"What about that pole?" William said. The pole designed to trigger the trap might have only covered a third of the chute's exit, but most of it had been attached to the wall above. "Can you tie it to the clothes to give us an extra five or six feet?"

Artan reached down for the large metal rod. He grunted as he wiggled it, but it didn't budge. Another tug and he got a small amount of play on it. When he pulled it one last time, the bar made a deep creak and came away from the wall, twanging as it shook from the release. While holding Max's hand to anchor himself, Artan leaned out and pulled the large metal basket back towards him, slamming it home with a loud *crash!*

The clothes rope, now weighted with metal, fell hard, the pole hurtling down. Fortunately they'd had the good sense to tie the pole in the middle of the rope so it didn't hit William. The bottom of the final pair of trousers—Artan's trousers—hung just one foot above him. William retrieved Ranger's sword, Jezebel, and Artan's war hammer. He tied the three weapons together, his voice echoing in the tight space. "Take these up first. We can't leave them here."

The weapons swayed on the rope. Like watching the glass cage, if one of them fell now, William would do well to avoid it. Jezebel protruded farther than the others, the scrape of her head against the wall. They'd blunt her if they weren't careful. But he kept it to himself. They were trying their best.

A couple more knocks before the weapons made it to the top and Artan sent the rope down again. The weapons had been a good test run. William pulled on it, lifting his feet from the ground. It took his weight.

A thirty-foot climb, William pressed his boots against the dark steel wall and began his ascent, inspecting each knot as he passed it.

At ten feet from the ground, the drop was only half what they'd fallen the first time, but if he fell now, it would be straight down rather than hitting a wall first. He also wouldn't have Artan to soften his fall.

"You're doing well, William," Cyrus said.

William pulled himself higher. Close to the chute's exit, he came to the pole as the next link in their makeshift rope. The pole slipped, William's body falling by an inch or two.

"William?" Artan this time.

His heart in his throat, William shook as he stared at the knot. Did he imagine it, or was it moving? The tightness seemed to be loosening, teasing him, toying with him, preparing to let him fall.

"What do you need us to do, William?" Max said.

The chute's exit in front of him, the basket still another ten feet above. The knot slipped again and William hung on, wrapping his legs around the rope, clinging on with all he had. Like that would help. A falling object was a falling object, no matter how hard he gripped it.

The fabric in the knot shifted again. The brown and black of the two garments moved like constrictors waking from sleep. "It's like Matilda always says," William muttered, "don't let your fear get in the way." He climbed higher and reached one hand into the chute, slapping it against the flat wall. Nothing to hold on to, it pushed him back, the entire rope taking him with it as it swung out over the pit. "Come on!"

Climbing higher, he kicked away from the wall again and uncrossed his legs, now entering the chute feet first. He spread his legs wide, using the soles of his boots to pin himself in place.

William's torso hung backwards from where he still held onto the rope. If he fell at that moment, the top of his skull would hit the ground first. He reached into the chute again.

The press of cold steel against his palm. Before he could bring his left hand in with it, the shifting knot came free.

In one move, William fell forwards and dragged the rope in with him. The effort of his struggle echoed in the tight chute as he lay against the cold steel and spread out like a star, pinning himself in place.

All of their trousers in his grip, William's legs shook and his breathing quickened. His eyes burned from the sweat running into them, and his shoulders buzzed with the cuts from the glass dust transferred from the bottom of the boys' boots. Biting down on the trousers freed his hands. He spread out in the chute, his left hand and foot bracing against the left wall, his right hand and foot against the right. He had this.

"William?" Max's voice echoed down the chute, assaulting him from all angles. "Are you okay?"

Other than a muffled reply because of the clothes in his teeth, William had nothing. Using his hands first, he reached up the chute before bracing and bringing his feet up behind. Several inches at a time, as long as he didn't slip, he'd get there.

Daylight at the top of the chute. He'd get there. Slow and steady.

"William!" Cyrus said. "We're going to send the rest of the rope down. If you can grab it, we'll drag you out."

Still as muffled, but closer so at least they'd hear him. "Have you taken that damn pole from it?"

"Yes."

The heavy knot at the end of the rope bounced down the chute and stopped inches from slamming into William's nose. His muscles on fire, his shaking body threatening to betray him, William braced his legs one last time and yelled out against his own fatigue as he boosted towards the knot.

Cyrus' face appeared at the end of the chute. "He has it. Pull!"

The first tug dragged William several feet. Although he tried to help them by pressing against the wall, they dragged him again before he could get a foothold. Other than his grip on the rope, William fell limp, his bare stomach scraping against the cold and rough steel.

Never so pleased to see a grinning Cyrus, William rolled over onto his back when he got to the top of the chute. The harsh wind instantly dried the sweat on his body, and his quivering returned. But better to be cold and alive. He smiled. "Thank you."

CHAPTER 11

The sun might have been setting, the day growing colder, but in their cave, sheltered from the wind, Olga leaned back against the wall and closed her eyes momentarily as she let the warmth that remained sink into her skin. Her entire body throbbed from everything they'd been through over the past day. The tall grass swayed, the meadow littered with large steel rocks. "I mean, there's a lot of steel out there, but apart from that, it doesn't look very different from the north."

While drawing long and deep breaths, Matilda faced the grassy wastelands, her eyes glazed.

"I suppose with this amount of steel," Olga said, "it makes sense they would have found inventive uses for it. Like constructing a wall. But what tools do they have over here? I just can't get my head around the logistics of creating something on this scale."

"I think I've seen enough of this side of the wall already," Matilda said.

"Oh." Olga straightened her back. "She speaks, then?"

"I think we should lie low in this cave for a little while longer, and then go back and find the boys."

"You don't think Magma's killed them by now?"

"I won't give up on them."

"I'm not asking you to."

"If I assume they're dead, that's as good as giving up on them."

The sun might have found them in the shadowy cave, but they couldn't enjoy its warmth for long. Olga shifted back into the darkness and Matilda followed. It kept them hidden from the diseased. The creatures had the object permanence of an infant. The second Mummy hides behind a door, they think they're alone. And a good job. Had it been any other way, they'd be dead by now. Twenty or so creatures remained below. Their squalls and shrieks had died to low rumblings of discontent. Occasionally one of them would snarl, stumble, and snap at the air around them as if the memory of the encounter with the girls remained. But they were confused outbursts at best. Maybe they'd already forgotten the girls and they were simply a symptom of the disease.

Olga shifted where she sat, the cold steel turning her bottom numb. "How long do you think we should wait?"

Matilda shrugged. "Thirty more minutes?"

"Hopefully Carl and Peter have killed each other back there."

"Thirty minutes should be enough time for us to find out."

"And it should give time for the diseased to clear off." Olga tightened her grip on Carl's knife. "And you know what? Whatever's ahead for us from here, at least we've managed to avoid Grandfather Jacks' community."

"That's a man I *never* want to meet."

A chill snaked through Olga. She shook her head to snap

out of it and snorted an ironic laugh. "I still can't get over Max and how he behaved. What a prick."

"I've known William for most of my life," Matilda said. "We were in school together from the age of six. There were many times where I assumed he hated me. It sounds cliché, but he used to pull my pigtails, bump into me in the playground, and tell me in no uncertain terms how gross girls were."

Olga smiled. "So when did he tell you he liked you?"

"I'm not sure he ever did. Certainly not while we were at school. He just wouldn't ever leave me alone." Tears glistened in her brown eyes. "One Valentine's Day I got home from school and he'd put a frog in my bag with a note. The frog had turned it so damp I could barely read what he'd written."

"What did it say?"

One blink sent a tear down each cheek, and Matilda smiled, her lips buckling when she spoke. "Can I be your handsome prince?"

Olga snorted a laugh. "Oh my god." She shook her head. "I think I would have kicked him in the nuts if he'd done that to me."

Matilda shifted, and the fading light caught the tracks of her tears. "I did. But my point is, boys can be awful communicators sometimes."

"But Max is *eighteen*."

"You give him too much credit. And of course there are many things that aren't acceptable, but not talking about how he feels … My mum used to tell me to give a boy until they're twenty-five before you expect them to be a man. If they're not done by then, you should walk."

"But—"

"It didn't work for her. I know. She always had great advice. If only she'd followed it herself."

Impossible to avoid the cold in their steel hole, Olga leaned back against the wall and reached out in front of her so her hands were in the splash of remaining sunlight. She placed Carl's knife on the ground before making fists and unclenching them. Red bands wrapped each wrist. They'd bound them too tightly. "It feels good to get those ropes off."

Before Olga could speak again, a female voice cut across the landscape. The low sun burned her eyes when she looked out over the grassy meadow. She snapped her hands away from the light. "How the hell did they get so close?"

About ten people were visible at first, several more popping up from the long grass. They were no more than thirty feet from the wall. All of them carried spears and they kept them raised. In their free hands they carried various weapons, from swords to bats to clubs. A roughly equal split of men and women, they all had long hair, with feathers, bones, and sticks tied in their braids, which hung down to their shoulders. A uniformity to their appearance, they wore trousers and waistcoats of different patches of animal skins stitched together. The whites and greys of rabbits, squirrels, and even the black and white stripes of badgers. A fine display of their hunting prowess.

The woman who'd spoken led the line. Pale, she had long blonde hair and ruddy cheeks. Although slight, she had toned arms. A tall man walked at her side. He had a slim waist, large biceps and broad shoulders. Darker skinned than the woman, he had a thick black beard. This group were clearly fit. They looked like they could run for days.

The woman screamed, a blood-curdling call that quickened Olga's pulse. She then released a shrill tongue roll before charging straight at the wall.

More hunters appeared as if they'd been birthed by their surroundings. Their number doubled and then tripled. They threw their spears as they ran. Like the hunters from Umbriel, they attacked with deadly accuracy, taking down at least half the pack of diseased with twenty feet still separating them.

The front runners split and pulled away to each side. Half of them went one way and half went the other. It opened a space for those at the back to throw their spears. The *whip* of the projectiles flew through the air. The *squelch* of them sank into the creatures.

The pack of diseased dispatched, the group walked over to them, retrieved their weapons, and examined the diseased's clothes. They took leather belts and smaller items. One of them relieved a diseased of their boots, pressing them against her own feet before she discarded the ones she wore and swapped them around.

"Do you think they're friendly?" Olga said while they picked over the diseased corpses.

"You want to risk it?"

"Dunno? Would it do us any harm to have some allies out here?"

"*If* they're allies. What if they're in with Grandfather Jacks?"

"Over half of them are women."

"So?"

"From what I gather, Grandfather Jacks isn't what you'd call a ladies' man. I'd imagine most women would like to see his head on a spike. Especially strong women like this. If we partner with them, they might get us out of here."

Matilda's cheeks sucked in from where she chewed the inside of her mouth. It added definition to her already high cheekbones. "I dunno. They can fight, there's no denying that, but I still think we're better on our own."

The group had moved quickly through the diseased. They'd stripped them of anything of value and now headed back the way they came.

"This is our last chance," Olga said.

Matilda shook her head. "It just doesn't feel right."

The group moved with a swagger. They were comfortable in the wastelands. How often did they get surprised by packs of diseased? Maybe they could have helped Olga and Matilda get away from their current situation. But maybe they would have handed them straight over to Grandfather Jacks.

When they were nearly out of sight, Olga said, "Do you think we just made a mistake?"

"I'd say so." The man's voice echoed in the deep cave.

Olga spun around. What little light remained in the cave caught the glint in Peter's feline eyes. He stepped forward from the shadows, from a tunnel that had been too dark to see. His face bloody and swollen, he grinned. Before Olga could reach for her knife, the echo of his punch rattled through her skull, her head bouncing against the cold steel ground. She gasped, her mouth filled with the coppery taste of her own blood, her ears ringing. Before she could get her words out, he punched her again.

CHAPTER 12

"It wasn't easy climbing out of that chute, you know?" Although William aimed the comment at Artan, he watched Cyrus in his peripheral vision. The boy's slumped shoulders lifted.

Artan clearly saw it too, the very hint of a smile raising one side of his mouth. "We would have been screwed if Cyrus hadn't made that rope. I should have got him to tie it to the pole; he would have done a much better job than me." He reached across and laid a hand on William's left shoulder. "Sorry about that."

William flinched as he imagined landing head first on the steel ground of the pit. "We're all still here, that's all that matters." They'd been walking for an hour or two along the valley carved into the massive steel wall. The day had grown long, the horizon a deep orange from the setting sun. The wind had picked up, forcing William to stoop against it, his ears and nose numb. It might have been more hazardous to travel in the dark, but if they tried to camp up here for the night, they'd freeze to death.

"I shouldn't have ever let Trent do what he did," Cyrus said. Before William could question it, the boy continued. "I went along with him. I let him …" He sighed. "I let him push people around who didn't agree with him."

"What—" But it only took a glance from Artan to silence William. Let the boy speak.

"Sure, we all saw what Magma was like when he came past us in the national service area. He slaughtered three people in front of us because they asked which direction they were heading in. But he also offered us a way out. We'd been on the roof of that hut for so long. And we were so hungry and thirsty."

"Don't beat yourself up," Artan said. "Most would have gone with him."

"But Jerry didn't want to." Cyrus' bottom lip buckled. "Jerry said he'd wait." He shook his head. "Trent wouldn't have that. In Magma he saw something to aspire to. He very publicly offered Jerry the chance to change his mind."

"And he didn't?" Artan said.

Cyrus' lips tightened. "And I didn't stick up for him. I saw it coming. When Trent asked Jerry to reconsider, the air shifted around us. It was like a thunderstorm was about to break. It only took for Jerry to …" Cyrus lost his words, running a hand over his short hair. "For Jerry to shake his head. Trent kicked him off the roof. I should have done more. I saw it coming and I watched."

"What could you have done?" William said.

All the while, Max hung back from the group and stared into the middle distance. He might have been with them in body, but his mind had gone somewhere entirely different.

Their feet tapping against the steel, the path stretched away from them as if it would never end.

"I've always been spineless," Cyrus said. "That's what

my mum called me. All the time. She said I wouldn't make it back from national service. That I didn't have it in me. She'd been saying that to me since I turned six."

"What did she know?" William said. "I'm proud to have you at my side."

A frown hooded Cyrus' confused eyes. "But what do I bring to this group?"

"You can climb," William said. "And you're light. God, I can't imagine having to be a human ladder for Trent. Or that stocky little Ranger."

Cyrus shrugged. He clearly didn't believe any of it. "How long do you think it'll be before we're off this damn wall? Do you think we'll get off before night?"

"And where are the girls now?" Artan said.

The clouds above had turned dark grey, burying the sunset. A mirror image of the steel wall they crossed, they promised one hell of a storm. William swallowed, his throat tacky with dehydration. He placed a hand on his rumbling stomach. "I'm guessing there isn't much deer hunting going on here either." He lifted Jezebel. "Not that I'd catch one with this."

"If you ever need someone to hold your war hammer while you hunt, Artan?" Max said.

"Oh my!" William paused at the top of another trap. "Good job this thing's already been triggered." A section of their path was depressed from where someone had already stood on it. "I'm not sure I would have seen the button in this light." A steep chute ran away from them. It had a dogleg in it. "That must have hurt to go round that bend."

Artan raised his eyebrows. "Not as much as hitting a wall and having your four friends land on top of you."

Cyrus had walked ahead of them. He came to a sudden

halt. "I'm sure she probably forgot how painful the chute was."

William joined the boy, his stomach knotting at the sight of the woman. She lay crucified on a bed of spikes in the pit at the end of the chute. The sharp gunmetal grey tips glistened with blood. One had gone through her throat, one through her eye, and one through her open mouth.

A shake of his head, Artan rubbed his chin. "She's not been dead long."

"Come on." William shuddered and led them away. "Let's keep moving. We can't do anything for her now."

The walls of the crevice grew gradually steeper as the path narrowed. It sharpened the already cutting wind. The sight of the woman had left a chill in William's bones, which the intensified weather did little to allay. He walked at the head of the line, Cyrus directly behind him, Artan at the back. The strong breeze obliterated his words before they'd left his mouth, but he didn't have the energy to shout. "How many people die trying to pass through here, I wonder."

Clunk! A section of wall about twenty feet wide dropped on their right. It revealed a cave filled with diseased. Cyrus screamed as the foetid reek of vinegar and rot rushed out, driven towards them on the back of the creatures' cries.

William lifted Jezebel. Artan the war hammer. Cyrus kept his sword sheathed and raised his hands as if he could push them away. He even closed his eyes. There were at least twenty diseased. Maybe more.

Max moved ahead of the group and pushed the diseased back. While he might have had disdain for the boy in the past, he stood mostly in front of the cringing Cyrus.

As the boys avoided the diseased, William noticed the *click* of the trap's trigger too late to act. His foot sank by an inch, and the wall behind them fell. The ground they stood on tilted like it had with the last trap.

Their yells echoing in the enclosed chute, all four of them slid away from the diseased.

The creatures followed them a second later.

Winded as he collided with a wall before falling to the floor of another pit, William threw Jezebel away from him for a second time so his friends didn't land on the axe. He'd already grown too used to this. Artan, Cyrus, and then Max slammed into him. A hole like the one they'd been in before, the walls as sheer and as tall.

William retrieved Jezebel and helped Artan to his feet.

The first of the diseased hit the wall like William had, the skeleton-jarring connection making him wince.

Just before Max stepped forward to attack it, Artan handed him his war hammer.

A devilish grin stretched across Max's face. He kicked the first diseased in the chest to prevent it from standing. He swung for the next one entering the pit, catching it with a full blow to the cheek. The hammer head sank into the thing's skull before it hit the ground. Max moved with a fluidity reminiscent of Warrior leaving the national service area ahead of the cadets. A ballet of destruction, he ended the diseased as they came down to him, slamming headshots as if the hammer carried no weight.

Jezebel raised, William maintained a tight grip on her handle while Cyrus held his sword in a shaking hand and Artan stood ready with his spear. But Max didn't need them. A frenzy of activity, he killed the diseased almost as quickly as they came to him, kicking some back before they overwhelmed him, and finishing them when they came at him a second time.

The bodies stacked up, William and the other two

pressing their backs to the wall of the pit to give Max the space he needed.

One of the creatures slipped through. Cyrus speared the beast in the face. Artan patted him on the back.

Although it had rained diseased, the flow stopped as quickly as it had started. For a second time, Cyrus drove his sword through a diseased, this time burying the tip in the back of its head. He panted as he said, "It moved."

With all the creatures down, William puffed his cheeks out as he exhaled. "Wow. Thanks, Max. And you, Cyrus."

A sheen of sweat glistened on Max's face, mixing with the blood from the diseased. Twenty or more bodies in front of them, he shook his head. "That was intense."

"You can say that—" The sound of voices above cut William off. Men's voices.

"Shit." Artan looked up. "They're nearby."

"What do we do?" Cyrus said.

Max pointed up. "We could try to climb out?"

"We won't make it," William said. The answer had already come to him, but he waited for something better from the others. After a pause, he said, "We need to hide."

"How do we hide in here?" Cyrus looked at the pile of diseased corpses. "Surely you don't mean …?"

The voices drew closer.

"There's no other choice," Artan said.

Max shook his head. "There must be another option?"

William said, "If there is, we have seconds to work it out."

Taking the lead, Cyrus ran to the pile of diseased near the wall. He grunted when he dragged several away from the mound and winced as he lay down and pulled the bodies over him. The others did the same.

The still-warm flesh pressed down on him. The funky

reek of curdled meat in his nostrils, his clothes turning damp with their warm blood, William swallowed against his still-dry throat while the others shifted around him and the voices above grew louder. In a matter of seconds, they'd be staring down at them. Hopefully they'd done enough to turn themselves invisible.

CHAPTER 13

A needle of hot agony ran from the side of Olga's head into her right eyeball. She dragged air in through clenched teeth and screwed her face up, another hot wave streaking through her. Her head strapped in place, she twisted against her restraints. Not only had a leather belt been pulled taut across her brow, but one had been strapped across her mouth, forcing her to breathe through her nose. Her arms were pinned to her sides and her legs bound so she lay dead straight on the wooden stretcher.

Barp! A tone in the distance. A horn of some sort.

Even blinking sent electric streaks through her face, but it cleared her vision, bringing definition to the silhouettes surrounding her. Three people on either side: two men and four women. They wore fur coats made from a mix of different animals. Rabbit, squirrel, wildcat. One of them had the black and white of a badger on their back. They all had long braided hair reaching down to their shoulders. Feathers, twigs, and bones had been twisted through the braids, some of them tinkling like wind chimes in the strong breeze.

The wooden stretcher bobbed with their steps, and they

talked amongst themselves. Olga heard everything as if she listened to it from underwater, fluid in her ears, the back of her throat coated with the coppery taste of her own blood.

Barp!

Olga clamped her jaw, sending stinging shocks up either side of her face. But screw the pain. She twisted against her bonds and shook again. The woman at the front of the stretcher stumbled with the movement.

A grin lit the face of one of the men, who peered down on her, the darkening sky surrounding him. It would be night soon. "She's awake."

The man moved aside to reveal a beaming Peter. He walked at the same pace as those carrying the stretcher. The familiar spread of his feline eyes, his smile a beaming white. Two more people joined him. A pale woman with blonde hair. Although slim, the definition of her arms spoke of her fitness. A tall man with dark features at her side. Flecks of grey dusted his thick black beard. When Olga had seen them from the cave, she'd not noticed the man's ageing. Crows' feet spread away from the corners of his ochre eyes; permanent wrinkles sat on his brow.

"Welcome back," Peter said. He then pointed at the woman and man. "This is Collette and Serj."

They both smiled and nodded like they were being introduced at a party. Like they didn't have her pinned to a fucking stretcher. Olga bucked, the woman at the front stumbling for a second time.

Barp!

"Careful," Peter said. "If they drop you, you'll come off much worse."

Snot rocketed from Olga's nose with her heavy breaths. As much as she tried to pull away from Peter's touch, she was powerless to the man stroking her face. His smile remained broad, his eyes losing focus as he stared down on her. He spoke in a hushed tone. "Now, now, my little thing. You had me so worried when you and your friend vanished earlier."

Matilda! Olga tried to turn her head. Millimetres of movement, nothing more.

"Show her," Peter said.

Barp!

Those carrying the stretcher tilted one side, and Olga's stomach lurched as if she might fall. But the straps held her so tightly she barely moved. In a similar situation to her, they had Matilda bound to another stretcher. Leather straps pinned her in place. Her eyes were currently closed.

"That's enough," Peter said. When the stretcher levelled out, he smiled again. "Don't worry, she's just resting. She'll be right as rain soon. Now I suppose you must be wondering where you're going, and who these people are?"

Had Olga been able to reply, she might have withheld it to deny him the satisfaction. But currently, she had no control.

"These people are nomads. They work for bounties and rewards. They know Grandfather Jacks and are sympathetic to his mission."

"We also like how well he pays," Collette added, laughing with Serj and Peter at the comment.

"They're helping me complete my mission of delivering you and your little friend to him. You should thank them for steering you through this tumultuous world. For taking an interest in your path to enlightenment."

Another tight clamp on her jaw, the stinging pain gave her something to focus on.

Barp!

A shriek from nearby diseased. Olga's heart accelerated, her breathing quickening. The swish of long grass as they closed in, she fought against her bonds.

Thwip. Thwip. Thwip. Three spears were loosed. The diseased fell silent.

"And as you can see," Peter said, "the nomads are handy when it comes to dealing with the diseased. Now show her where we're going."

Those at the back of the stretcher lifted it to give Olga a view of what lay ahead. They were no more than fifty feet from a huge, imposing, and windowless building. Tall, wide, and made from large grey stones, it dominated the landscape. Bigger than any building she'd ever seen, it must have had hundreds of rooms inside. A rock of dread plummeted through her stomach.

Barp! The sound came from the other side of the building.

They lowered the back of the stretcher again, forcing Olga to view the darkening sky. Night just a few hours away. Although, from the look of the building, the light would be taken away from her much sooner.

The groaning of old hinges up ahead, they carried Olga into a tunnel made from an intricate latticework of steel. Complex filigree. She'd seen similar pattens in some of the wooden furniture in Edin. Beautiful artistry, such care given to something leading to somewhere so remarkably ugly.

The crashing of closing gates. The screech of diseased. Not only did the tunnel display gothic beauty, but it held the creatures back, several of them slamming into the fences on either side. The wet *schlop* of sharp points sank into rancid flesh as the nomads despatched them. The vinegar reek of stuck diseased swept across Olga's nose, riding on the back of the strong wind.

Barp!

Like they'd seen in the main hut in Umbriel, glass suns ran along the top of the tunnel when they got closer to the main building. Smaller and duller, but more numerous. Every few feet, two sat centrally above her like glowing yellow cherries. Where did this magic come from?

The tunnel stretched ten to twenty feet long. A loud snap ran through Olga. A bolt being freed. Another yawning groan of protesting hinges. The latticework overhead was replaced by a solid roof. Shadows crawled through the deep corridor, but more small glass suns clung to the walls on either side. Their dull glow created more shadows than they banished.

Barp! The loud noise roared through the building, shaking the walls, echoing along the corridors. It shook Olga's chest and snapped her rigid. Peter walked on as if nothing had happened.

Ten to fifteen seconds later. *Barp!*

Again, none of the others reacted.

The shadows deepened when the doors slammed shut behind them. Nothing but the glow from the weak suns on either side. The place had a musty reek of damp.

Barp!

A woman screamed. It came from somewhere deep inside the building, the lonely call searching the corridors for someone. Anyone.

Two to three turns later and Olga had already lost track of where they'd taken her. A maze of corridors, the ceiling the same no matter how many turns they made. Even when she did get free, how would she find her way out?

Barp!

Another scream, it came from another distant room. Peter laughed. "That's the sound of transition. Soon they'll see the way to Grandfather Jacks. Soon they'll find the peace they deserve. And when they do"—he pressed his hands together in prayer—"they'll thank us for opening their eyes. They all do in the end."

Those carrying the stretcher stopped. *Crack!* Another bolt

opened. More old and protesting hinges. Another door swung wide.

They pushed Olga into a dark cell. They leaned her against the wall, bringing Matilda in and standing her beside her. Vertical or horizontal, the bonds continued to pin her in place.

Peter pressed his hands together for a second time and addressed the ceiling. "High Father, I'm honoured to deliver this gift to you. Two more pure souls desperate for a leading light in this dark, dark world. Please accept them as your own. We trust you will deliver them to a higher consciousness and show them how you provide. How wonderful life can be under your guidance."

Grinning like he had the entire time, Peter walked backwards from the room, his attention shifting from Matilda to Olga as if waiting for enlightenment to burst from them. He vanished from their view and called back into the room, "Enjoy your new cellmates."

The next *barp* drowned out the slamming door. Most of the light in the room vanished.

The shadows came to life. One, two, then three silhouettes. They moved slowly forwards, their footsteps clumsy as they slapped against the ground. Canted stances. One of them dragged a back foot as if its leg no longer worked.

The small room threw Olga's quickened nasal breaths back at her. Gagged by the leather strap, she grunted a muffled scream and shook her head as much as the millimetres of movement would allow.

The three silhouettes drew closer.

Barp!

Matilda remained unconscious. The only movement she had in her arms, Olga wriggled her fingers. The three people were nearly in the small splash of light from the weak yellow sun on the wall.

Barp!

A warm dampness spread across Olga's thighs as she lost control of her bladder.

CHAPTER 14

Jezebel at his side, William lay beneath the press of fast-cooling diseased bodies. A small stone dug into his right shoulder blade, hitting a pressure point that forced all the muscles in his back to spasm. As slowly as he could, he shifted his weight. Enough to move off the stone, but hopefully not so much anyone looking down would have perceived it. A cold dead hand rested against his right cheek. Bloody red eyes stared at him through the gaps in the fingers. His change in position had afforded him a clearer view of the top of the pit. The sky had grown darker from where night closed in, the strong wind whistling across the mouth of the wide hole. The men closing in on the pit were yet to make themselves visible.

Cyrus lay on William's right, another body among many, although none of the diseased trembled like him. Max lay on his left, dead still as if he welcomed the inaction. He could finally give in to the hopelessness of screwing over Olga and watching her kiss Hawk. Artan lay close to Cyrus.

The stench, William could get used to. Time around these vile creatures had taught him he could become accustomed to almost any reek. Eventually his senses would dull. But their weight pressing down on him … The very tangible pressure of the vile things squashing him, leaning on him. So close. So intimate.

"I don't fucking believe it," Max said beneath his breath.

William turned too fast and one of the bodies on top of him slid by a few inches. The staring diseased fell away to be replaced with the crotch of another one. Previously a man. If he'd had a choice between the two, he would have opted for the crimson glare. The voices had taken form, several hunters appearing at the edge of the pit. The broad and scarred Hawk stood among them.

"Where did that fucking prick come from?"

"Now's not the time, Max," William said. "If they realise we're down here, we're screwed. It's going to be hard enough working out how we get out of this pit without spears raining down on us."

"But of all people …"

"I'm lying here with a diseased's dick in my face, so believe me when I say, if there was a way to get out of here and move on, I'd be with you. But there isn't. We need to wait for them to go."

Another boy joined the gang at the edge of the pit. The tall kid who'd won the chance to go out hunting the first time William and the others attempted Umbriel's spear-throwing trial. Naked from the waist up—as all of them were—his pecs stood out as two rocks on his chest, his stomach a rippled six-pack. He freed himself from his trousers and groaned as he pissed on the diseased.

William pressed his mouth shut and closed his eyes. Some of the spray from the boy landed pinpricks of moisture against him, although the layer of diseased on top took most of it. A secondary warm trickle ran across William's thighs, dampening his trousers.

"Looks like someone had some fun here," one of the other hunters said, a short ginger kid, nearly as broad as he was tall. "Although ... how did the diseased die?"

Cyrus snapped tense beside William, several of the corpses shifting. He let out the faintest whine.

"Keep it together," William said. "They've not seen us yet. Just keep your head."

Hawk shrugged. "They fell in there."

"How do you work that out?" the ginger kid said.

"Look at the impact wounds to their heads. How else would that happen if they didn't fall?" Hawk's stamp sent a ringing across the top of the pit. "This steel's unforgiving when you take a swan dive onto it from a great height."

One of the other boys called at those gathered around the hole, "I think we should stay here until morning. We have deer that need skinning and eating, and we don't have to be at Grandfather Jacks' community for another two nights. I don't know about you lot, but I don't fancy getting there early, and with an hour or two before it's completely dark, I think we need to pick a spot soon anyway."

"How much longer is the walk to the community?" the boy who'd urinated into the pit said. The new boy, he probably had many similar questions.

"Half a day from here. I mean, we'll need to catch some more deer before we turn up, but that still gives us plenty of time. Also, up here, we're much less likely to run into the diseased."

The boy who'd pissed pointed down into the pit.

"I said much *less* likely. Not that we wouldn't."

"How many do you think are up there?" Cyrus said.

Although he aimed his reply at the nervous boy, William

said it loud enough for Max to hear. "Too many. I want to get to Matilda and Olga more than anything else, but we have no choice but to wait for them to go."

"Maybe we can wait for them to go to sleep and then move?" Max said.

Cyrus' voice trembled. "I'd rather wait for them to move on like William said. They'll be bound to have someone on guard all night."

William said, "It seems like the only sensible choice, Max."

"But they're bedding down for the rest of the day and night," Max said.

William's stomach rumbled. Even with the diseased corpses pressing down on him, he'd kill for some deer meat right now. "And it looks like we are too."

"Artan?" Max said, many of the hunters moving away from the edge of the pit. "What do you say?"

"I agree with William. I hate it as much as you all do, but I don't see any other option."

Pins and needles buzzed in William's right arm. He shifted again to relieve the pressure.

CHAPTER 15

The only power afforded to her, Olga repeated the same useless action of clenching her jaw and twisting against her restraints. Her trousers clung to her thighs, the cold air adding a chill to the damp fabric. The loud, wall-shaking *barp* matched the three silhouettes' next step, all of them coming forward in a wave. The one dragging its foot had support from the person next to them.

Barp!

A small splash of light from the tiny sun on the wall revealed the first of the three people. Dianna! The girl from Umbriel. The two girls behind her were the stocky one Rayne had dragged from the tunnel when she and William had been outside Magma's fortress, and the other one, the girl from the fire in Magma's community, the one with mousy-brown hair. Smaller and slighter than the one from the tunnel, the mousy-brown girl dragged her right leg behind her, her foot limp as if her ankle had been shattered. Where the slight girl had previously looked out on the world with fear, she now wore a blank stare. She must have been in agony, but her gaunt face and hollow eyes showed she'd gone to another place. A numb existence beyond pain.

Barp!

Dianna came closer to the girls. An apologetic wince, she untied the strap gagging Olga.

Olga gasped, spreading her mouth wide to inhale the damp and chilly air. She filled her lungs and let it out again.

Matilda's eyes opened when Dianna released the strap across her mouth.

Barp!

"What the hell is that sound?" Olga said.

Dianna tossed the leather straps to the floor. "You get used to it. Either that or it sends you nuts."

As if on cue, the mousy-brown girl pressed her hands together in prayer. "Grandfather Jacks provides."

While working her jaw, Matilda blinked repeatedly. Her voice weak, she said, "And that's its only purpose? To drive us insane?"

"We are in the asylum," Dianna said. "The sound calls the diseased to the other side. It means Grandfather Jacks—"

"Praise be to the High Father," the mousy-brown girl said in a monotone voice.

Dianna rolled her eyes. "It means Grandfather Jacks and anyone working for him can enter the asylum through the tunnel at the back much more easily."

Barp!

The sound shook Olga to her core as if it had a direct line to her very being. "But how do they make such a loud noise? And where do all the glass suns come from? You had one in Umbriel. What kind of magic is it?"

The girl with the mousy-brown hair stepped closer. She put most of her weight on her broken ankle, her expression unchanged as her foot buckled beneath her. "It all comes from the High Father. He's pulled them down from heaven and given them to Grandfather Jacks. It's the glow that lights our path towards salvation."

Although the stocky girl from the tunnel hadn't spoken, she wore the same sceptical frown as Dianna.

"It's electricity," Dianna said, quietly enough to not distress the brown-haired zealot.

"It's *what?*" Olga said.

"Electricity. Power. We can power lights, heat rooms, cook food." *Barp!* Dianna sighed. "Make really annoying sounds. Electricity is a wonderful thing. We use something called solar power. They're large black panels that take the sun's energy and change it into something we can use."

Barp!

After a few seconds, Dianna wrung her hands in front of herself. "Um … Did the boys make it?"

"You know what happened to them?" Matilda said.

"They were handed over to Magma, right?"

A surge of energy raced through Olga and she lurched forwards. At least, she attempted to. Her restraints kept her pinned to the wooden stretcher. "If you knew what was going to happen to them, why didn't you tell us?"

"I only found out when they were bringing me here. By then they'd already separated us."

"But you knew about this place?"

"Everyone in Umbriel does."

"And you didn't think it was worth sharing with us?" Olga spat as she spoke. "A friendly heads-up could have helped us get away before this happened."

"They said they'd kill us if we told you. And not just us, they'd kill everyone we cared about too. They threatened to kill Rita and Mary if I said anything. I lost my family in the wild lands a long time ago …" The glass sun's weak light caught the spread of tears in Dianna's eyes. "Those two women have been like mothers to me since they took me in. I'm sorry, but I couldn't put them in harm's way."

"So instead you let the boys die and allowed them to bring us here?" Olga said.

Dianna's tears broke and ran down her cheeks. She shook her head and bit her quivering lip. "I hope they found a way out of it."

Olga said, "You think that makes up for it?"

Dianna dropped her attention to the stone floor. The girl might have been strong and carried herself with confidence, but she couldn't have been any older than fourteen.

"They had Max with them," Matilda said. "That has to give us some hope."

Barp! The sound continued, every ten to twenty seconds.

They couldn't blame Dianna for this. The men had to answer for their actions, not a fourteen-year-old girl. "So," Olga said, chewing her tongue for several seconds. She took a breath to calm the fire in her gut. "What is this place? What's going to happen to us?"

After a slight pause, Dianna looked up again. "This is where we get *conditioned* in preparation for Grandfather Jacks. We're taught how to become his brides."

The girl with the mousy-brown hair said, "And praise be to the High Father for such a generous gift." She stepped forward another pace, the weak sun revealing the swirling madness in her distant glare. "Grandfather Jacks is the only one among us who hears the message from the High Father. He's the conduit who delivers enlightenment to our community. And he's been blessed with the ability to help girls transition into womanhood."

The leather strap across Olga's brow prevented her from shaking her head. Dianna stepped closer and began untying her bonds. "What the hell is that lunatic talking about?" Olga said.

"On the full moon," Dianna said, "he marries us and provides us with our first *adult* experience."

"When's the next full moon?"

"In two nights' time."

"Screw that!"

Where the mousy-brown girl had spoken in monotone, her voice now shook and her face reddened. "It's a blessing. A gift from the High Father. It allows us to be ready for motherhood and families. It's a great honour."

"I'll tear his throat out if he comes anywhere near me."

The girl shook when she screeched, "It's his job!" Her teeth clenched; her eyes locked onto Olga with the focus of a predator. "It's what he has to do for the good of the community."

"*You* might think it's for the good of the community," Olga said, "but it sure as hell ain't good for me." Dianna untied the strap across her upper body. Olga rolled her shoulders, a twinge sending a numb throb down her right arm.

The girl from the tunnel took the one with the broken ankle back into the darkness. Dianna finished untying Olga.

While Dianna worked on Matilda, Olga checked the cell door. A small barred window no more than a foot square in the centre of it. It seemed pointless, but she snapped the handle down and tugged. The door didn't budge.

Barp!

A woman screamed, the tormented yell quickening Olga's pulse.

Matilda now free, Dianna said, "There's no way out of here. We've checked."

Olga joined Dianna and Matilda. The girls Rayne had brought to the asylum were well and truly gone. They were loyal to Grandfather Jacks. Loyal to the point of hostility. But they weren't the enemy. Although they were hidden by the shadows, Olga nodded in their direction and spoke beneath her breath. "I won't let that happen to me. I'll die before I give in to him."

"You might well have to," Dianna said.

"No way." Olga shook her head. "I'm going to show this faux prophet what happens when you push too far. Only one of us is walking away from this, and it won't be him."

CHAPTER 16

The corpse on top of William twitched, and he woke with a start, his first conscious breath of the morning a deep inhalation of the creature's foetid reek. Another diseased shifted, this time the one covering his legs. Already alert enough to stifle his reaction, William blinked away the fog of sleep, the brightness of a new day stinging his tired eyes.

Another shifting corpse, this one farther away. Its movement rippled through the carpet of cold bodies pressing down on them. William's sight cleared, the silhouettes at the edge of the pit taking form as they threw more deer bones on top of them, each one sending a shimmer through the densely packed cadavers.

"Shall we kick the fire in?" one of the hunters called.

Hawk—the loudest voice, maybe because William recognised it—said, "No. I tell you what, if someone's made it this far through the funnel without a map, then they deserve to be heated by a still-burning fire. Good luck to them, I say."

"What would Grandfather Jacks say?"

"Grandfather Jacks doesn't need to know, does he? It's not like he ever leaves his palace."

An early morning dew coated everything, including the corpses. Their clothes were damp enough to transfer the moisture to William below. The steel like a block of ice against his back, the morning air had a bite to it. He drew shallow breaths to keep the condensation he exhaled to a minimum.

Pins and needles now in his left leg, William gritted his teeth against the highly sensitised buzz throbbing through it. Bad enough before he'd gone to sleep the previous evening, but lying beneath their dead press all night had made the sensation a thousand times worse. He wriggled his toes, which sent a tingle directly into his groin.

Despite the rancid diseased reek of vinegar, rot, and human waste, the aroma of roasting deer still found its way to William. His stomach resumed where it had left off the previous evening, rumbling like a growling beast.

How far away were the girls now? Had the old hunters kept moving with them? If William and the others were only half a day's walk from Grandfather Jacks' community, were they already there? But what could they do about it right now other than wait for the hunters to move on? To reveal themselves would be suicide. Better they got to the girls late than never.

The apparently reanimating diseased had demanded all of William's attention, but now he knew the reason for their twitching, the shivering Cyrus took his focus. Paler than usual, he trembled where he lay. Flat on his back on the grey steel, his eyes glazed.

"He's been trembling like a shitting dog for hours," Max said. "None of us can get him to stop. He'll blow our cover."

"Come on, Cyrus," Artan's soft voice called from the other side of the boy. "They can't wait up there forever. The second we get our chance, we'll climb out of this hellhole."

"Y-y-you promise?"

"Of course. But you need to wait, okay? You need to try to relax."

"Relax?"

"Shhhh!" Artan said. "Keep your voice down."

Before William had fallen asleep, they'd plotted their route out of the pit. The walls were nowhere near as sheer as they'd first seemed. Crags and lumps along the surface gave them a trackable path to the top. Now they needed to wait for the hunters to go.

"It won't be long now," Artan said.

Max nudged William, several diseased shifting on top of them. The crotch he'd faced the previous evening had gone. The open mouth of an old woman with deep gashes in her sallow cheeks now offered him a silent scream. "He's been like this all night. I don't know how you slept through it."

"I sleep like the dead," William said.

"I can see that."

"Sorry." William rolled his eyes. "Bad metaphor."

"Some would say appropriate."

Several more deer bones flew into the pit, one of them giving off a hollow knock as it connected with the back of the woman's head leaning over William. "That has to be a good thing though, right?" William said.

"As long as we don't get taken out by one of the bones," Max said.

"But at least it looks like they're packing up to move on."

"Here's hoping."

The bodies then shifted to William's right. Cyrus sat up first, Artan a second later as he grabbed the boy and slammed him back down on his back. "Wait!" Artan hissed, his face red as he leaned just inches from Cyrus. "Not yet."

"Leave that!"

The words from above snapped William rigid. It sounded like Hawk.

Artan dragged several corpses over him and Cyrus.

A hunter replied, "But there's a half-eaten deer here."

"We'll catch more later." After a slight pause, the shuffle of feet moved off, many of the hunters walking away from the pit. "We need to arrive at Grandfather Jacks' with offerings," Hawk continued. "You think he wants to chow down on our leftovers? Also, who knows how he'll react if he finds out we ate before arriving. He might decide this was one of his deer and we've caused great offence both killing and eating it without his permission. The man thinks *everything* belongs to him."

"I feel sorry for those girls in the asylum," one of the other hunters said.

William's entire body snapped rigid.

Hawk sighed. "Me too."

"Asylum?" Max said.

William shook his head. "I was hoping I'd heard them incorrectly."

"And what about us?" the hunter talking to Hawk said. He spoke with a nasally whine.

"What about us?"

"We could do with having something to munch on while we hike."

"You're not full from last night? Look, we're only half a day away. You know Grandfather Jacks will treat us like princes when we get to his palace. The last thing we should do is arrive with our bellies full. Stop being a prick and leave the deer where it is."

"What if someone finds it?"

"Good luck to them," Hawk said. "Like with the fire, if someone's made it this far into the funnel from either side, they deserve a little reward. Getting here without knowing where all the traps are is no mean feat."

The diseased on William's right moved again. Artan pulled Cyrus down for a second time.

"Artan," Max hissed, "if you can't stop him, I will."

The same mild tone, Artan said, "Hold it together, Cyrus. Not long now, mate. Just give it a few more seconds."

"Come on," Hawk called back across the pit. The rest of the hunters had already walked away.

The slap of the last hunter's feet finally took off after Hawk and the others.

The deceased diseased on William's right lifted and toppled onto him. Cyrus had gotten to his feet again, and Artan hadn't stopped him this time.

"Fuck it," William said. "Let's go now." As he stood up, Artan and Max stood up on either side of him. Each of them were covered in the bloody slime excreted by the weeping corpses. A crimson sludge so dark and clotted it looked like blackberry jam.

Cyrus took to the wall first.

William plunged his hand back into the diseased bodies like a morbid lucky dip. He shifted around until he found her wooden handle. Jezebel glistened like the rest of them, but at least he had her. His feet twisting and turning as he walked over the bodies, he slipped the handle down the back of his shirt, the axe's blade leaning against the back of his head.

They'd judged it correctly from the ground. The walls out of there were covered in lumps and cracks, places for their hands and feet so they could scale away to freedom.

His limbs still dead from where they'd been crushed all night between the heavy bodies and the hard cold steel, William shook by the time he reached the halfway point. The metal wall icy to touch, a thin layer of dew threatened to coax his fingers free.

"What are you doing?" Hawk shouted.

All four of the boys froze.

"I need a piss." The same nasal tone of the hunter who'd tried to take the deer meat and extinguish the fire.

"So take a piss, then."

Max on one side of him, Artan on the other. Cyrus had climbed several feet higher. They all clung to the wall like petrified lizards.

"That's what I'm doing," the hunter said.

"Here, I mean," Hawk said. "You've already held us up longer than you've needed to."

"I get stage fright."

The colour drained from Artan's cheeks. Everything had gone wrong the night he needed to urinate in private. Were it not for his shyness, he wouldn't have walked down into the ruins and Magma wouldn't have found him. Although he probably would have gotten them eventually.

"What kind of a man are you?" Hawk leered. "You can't even take a piss in public? Had we known that, we would have left you practicing on the scaffolding until you had the stones to join us."

William's fingers ached from where he clung to the wall. The tips numb from the cold, the tendons burned, threatening to spasm. He touched Jezebel's axe head with the back of his own. If he needed to, he'd be able to grab her. For what good it would do halfway down the pit. They had to get to the top. If they had even a slim chance of survival, they needed to be on level ground. He climbed several more feet, the others copying him.

The hunter whined his response. "Just let me take a leak."

"I'm not stopping you. But do it there."

"You don't get what it's like. You're lucky."

"Stop being a little girl."

Several other hunters joined in.

"You need to man up," one of them said.

Another one added, "I bet you sit down when you wee, don't you?

"Want me to hold it for you?"

The boy's voice broke from the force of his shout. "You lot are pricks, you know that?"

They laughed and clapped while they chanted, "Do it, do it, do it."

William led the others in climbing higher.

"Fucking hell!" the hunter shouted.

A drum roll of footsteps from where the boys ran on the spot. They made a low tone, a collective roar of encouragement that grew in volume. They then erupted with cheers and clapping. Many of them laughed.

Now closer to the top of the pit, William focused on his breaths in an attempt to forget about his aches.

"Happy?" the hunter finally said. His voice grew fainter as he headed back towards them and repeated, "You lot are fucking arseholes."

Just feet from the top of the pit, William now in the lead, he checked behind. Max, Artan, and Cyrus all nodded at him. They could wait for a short while. They needed to wait. The pasty complexion of panic had left Cyrus. His breaths came with a solid regularity. Somehow, they'd gotten through this.

A minute or two later, William poked his head over the lip of the hole. The hunters were gone. He climbed up, falling flat against the damp and cold steel. Thick rain clouds had moved in and blocked the sun.

When Artan climbed up, he hugged Cyrus. "Well done."

Swollen bags sat beneath Cyrus' eyes. "For what? Panicking?"

Artan had slid the handle of his war hammer down the back of his shirt like William had with Jezebel. He removed his weapon. "You held it together."

"You held it together for me."

"We need to support each other."

Max patted Cyrus' back. "Well done, mate. That wasn't easy."

Cyrus' mouth fell wide. For a second he said nothing. He then nodded. "Thank you."

Max shrugged and turned away from the boy. "How much of a prick is Hawk?"

"But we already knew that," William said.

Max raised an eyebrow.

"At least he left that behind." Artan pointed at the still-glowing fire beside the pit. The back leg of a deer was suspended over it, with most of the meat still on the bone.

"I say we eat it and then move on," William said. "Who knows where the girls are now; a few more minutes to stop and eat probably won't make much difference."

"I'd say they're already with Grandfather Jacks. And you heard the hunters, we're only half a day's walk from them. The full moon's tomorrow night. We have time."

"Although," Cyrus said, "what's the asylum?"

The question took the air from William's lungs and he shook his head. "It sounds awful, whatever it is. And for Hawk to say he pitied them being in there …"

"Olga and Matilda are strong," Artan said. "Let's sit down and eat. It'll take ten to fifteen minutes at the most. After that we can move on. It will also give the hunters more time to get away. The last thing we want to do is run into them again."

CHAPTER 17

Barp!

"My *God!*" Olga said, stamping her foot. "I thought I'd get used to that sound." Although, by the way Dianna twitched every time it went off, if anything, it would grow increasingly harder to bear.

It had been hours since Dianna had freed them. The broken girl with the broken ankle and her stocky and less vocal friend remained in the shadows. Maybe they were sleeping, or maybe they'd been watching them all night, gathering information to feed to their saviour, the High Father.

Barp!

Tiredness burned Olga's eyes. She'd not slept a wink. The weak glow from the small sun gave her enough light to encourage her to try to make out her surroundings, but not enough for her investigations to yield any effective results. Maybe they were well and truly trapped. Maybe she simply couldn't see the way out.

A loud *crack* followed by yet another *barp!* A small hatch opened in the bottom of the door. A metal plate about six inches in diameter shot through the space like a puck. The first time Dianna had moved in hours, she trapped it with her right hand and passed it to Matilda.

The next plate shot through Olga's legs as she made her way towards the door. Dianna trapped that one too.

Whoever fired the plates into the room were careful enough not to poke their hands through. Olga imagined grabbing their wrists and pulling them, repeatedly slamming their head against the other side of the door until she knocked them unconscious.

The third plate shot in. Then the fourth. After the fifth, the hatch snapped shut. "Damn it," Olga said, her face pressed to the door's metal bars. So dark outside, she could only make out the back of the retreating silhouette.

Dianna tucked into the food and spoke with her mouth full, her cheeks bulging as she waved her metal spoon like a wand. "This place might be hell on earth, but the food's always been good."

The girls in the corner were clearly awake, the clink of metal on metal as they tucked into their meal. Matilda hadn't started yet. She shifted forward so the light from the dull sun shone on her face. Her eyes wide, she shrugged.

"If they're eating it …" Olga said.

A red sauce, chunks of gamey meat, and something doughy beneath it. The tomato's acidity made Olga's mouth water. Although she ached from head to toe from their journey, the cramps in her stomach eased a little at the prospect of food. "What is it?"

"Pasta," Dianna said. "It's made from wheat. The sauce is deer meat and chopped tomatoes."

"It's good."

"I told you."

"I'll eat their food," Olga aimed her voice at the two spies in the corner, "but that doesn't mean I'm prepared to take their bullshit."

Matilda spoke with her mouth full. "We just need to pick the right time."

"But if I don't fight everything," Olga said, "how do I test for cracks?" She turned to Dianna. "What's your plan?"

The young girl shrugged. "I don't see how I'm in a position to make any plans."

The stone floor might have been warm compared to the funnel, but it still turned Olga's bottom numb. She shifted to get more comfortable and sniffed a wet sniff, her sinuses clogged with the cloying damp funk in the air. "Whether we formulate a plan or not, I promise you we're going to find a way out of here. I will not take this." The two in the corner had clearly heard them, so Olga turned their way. "And what about you?"

"Grandfather Jacks provides."

"Not you, I can see you're all in. You?"

"Me?" the girl with the black hair said.

"Yeah, you. What's your name?"

"Heidi."

"What's your plan, Heidi?"

A small voice in the dark, Heidi clearly hadn't lost the plot yet. "Honestly, I don't see that I have any other choice but to go ahead with this."

"That's bullshit." Olga flinched when Matilda touched her leg. Maybe she should go easier on this girl, but maybe now wasn't the time to be masking the truth. "If you let men tell you your place in this world, then you've already given up."

"But if I get this over and done with," Heidi said, "I can go to Umbriel and be safe. Maybe it's a price worth paying."

"You see an oppressive existence in Umbriel as the prize? Have you seen how the women are treated there? They're expected to make babies and do all the hard graft. I'd rather live among the diseased."

Heidi's voice grew even fainter. "Not all of us are cut out for fighting the diseased."

"And you understand what Grandfather Jacks plans to do to you? How old are you?"

"Fifteen."

"You're a kid. This shouldn't be happening."

"If I get it over and done with, the torture will stop. I can move on."

She'd already been too hard on the girl. How could Olga blame her for making the best bad choice? Maybe getting through this and getting out would give her more of a chance in this world. But … she shuddered, who the hell did Grandfather Jacks think he was?

Yet another wall-shaking *barp!*

Crack! The lock on the door snapped open. Olga placed her food on the stone floor and stood up.

A haunting groan from the old hinges. In an attempt to loosen the tension in her body, Olga swayed from side to side. She rolled her shoulders and bounced on her toes. The others in the cell might have given up, but she wouldn't. No way. Never. Matilda got to her feet and stood beside her.

Five guards entered one after the other. Each carried a pole. They spread out, the small sun catching their scowling faces. There were three men and two women. All of them had wide, well-fed frames. The women both stood about five and a half feet tall, the men closer to six feet.

"What the hell?" Olga said. "What's with you two?" Matilda put a hand on her arm, but Olga pulled away and stepped closer to the guards. "You're a part of this patriarchal bullshit? How can you get behind that dirty old man and what he does to little girls? Well, unlike you two, I will not give up on what it is to be a woman." She jabbed her thumb into her chest. "I will not abandon my morals."

Matilda stepped forward and spoke beneath her breath. "I'm with you every step of the way, but you can't fight everything."

"I can fight these arseholes."

A fizz and crackle, the end of each guard's pole lit up, vivid blue bursting from the darkness.

Dianna remained seated, but she shifted back into the shadows. "You need to get away from them."

Olga shook her head and raised her fists. "They will *not* beat me."

The blue light dragged traces through the air when one of the guards swiped it at Olga. It had clearly been designed to distract, but she wouldn't fall for it. She ducked the next one and moved inside her attacker's guard.

A hard buzzing crackle, Olga's entire back spasmed when one of the guards came at her from the side. She lost control of her limbs, her arms snapping and twitching, her legs shaking before they gave out and threw her to the hard ground. Another blue light pressed into the side of her neck, and her vision blurred. Her jaw snapped and she bit her tongue, damn near choking on the coppery flow of blood running down the back of her throat. When the third pole pressed against her thigh, she pissed herself for a second time, her body flipping on the hard stone like popping corn.

The *barp* came through as they pinned her snapping and bucking body to the ground with their magic. Zero control over her actions, Olga's ears rang as her head repeatedly slammed against the stone floor. The ringing grew more distant as darkness closed in. Everything faded away.

CHAPTER 18

William ran his hand over the top of his head, his hair soft from where the thick stubble of his crewcut had grown out. They'd been walking for about half an hour, the grey clouds above threatening rain. When a large drop landed on his head, he said, "At last."

Artan walked at the front of their line. He turned back and raised an eyebrow. William pointed at the sky. "Rain!" Another drop landed on his head. Then another. Then another.

As the rain grew heavier, William rubbed his hands over his head again, cleaning the diseased funk from his hair and then his face. He looked up at the sky and let it fall onto his tongue. The slightly muddy taste of rainwater drove away the gamey tang of deer meat and dehydration.

The other boys did the same as they walked along the deep ravine in the steel mountain. The walls ran up into the sky on either side at a gradient too steep to climb, especially now they glistened with rainwater. Even their path turned slick, William's feet sliding once or twice with his progress.

Jezebel slung over one shoulder, William kept a hand free

to soften his fall should he slip. Artan maintained a two-handed grip on his war hammer. Maybe he trusted his balance more than William did.

Cyrus walked behind Artan, and Max took up the rear, his face locked in its usual scowl, his lips pursed. The narrow path prevented them walking side by side. Artan halted up ahead. A pit down to his left, narrower than the one they'd been in with the diseased but just as deep.

Filled with rocks, it took William a second to see the leg protruding from beneath the landslide. "He doesn't look like he's been dead long."

While letting out a long sigh, Artan scratched his head. "At least it means they haven't had time to re-arm the trap. Better him than us." He moved off.

Cyrus remained rooted to the spot, staring down into the pit. William gave him a gentle nudge to encourage him forwards. The man in the pit hadn't stood a chance. Some of the rocks were large enough to take a life on their own. So many had rained down on him, they'd all but buried him. Less keen eyes could have been forgiven for missing the man there at all.

For the second time in as many minutes, Artan halted. The wash of rain slammed down on them, cleaning away any trace of the diseased. William leaned around Cyrus. "Artan, what's going on?"

Artan spun around, his finger pressed to his lips.

Were the rain not hammering his surroundings, William would have heard it much sooner. Holding Jezebel with both hands, he skirted around Cyrus and closer to Artan. "The hunters?"

Artan nodded.

"How far away?"

The path ahead of them bent around to the right. Artan shrugged. "Twenty feet. At the most."

"Shall we climb up there?" Cyrus pointed at the wall on their right. A slightly gentler slope than that on their left, it led to a ledge about ten feet above. It would have been a challenge scaling the dark steel in the dry, let alone now.

"They're ahead of us," William said.

Cyrus shrugged. He didn't understand.

"They have no reason to come back this way. They're heading to Grandfather Jacks' community. We just need to wait it out and we'll be fine. We need to give them a chance to move on."

William passed Artan, who grabbed his arm in a tight grip, his eyes wide. When William dipped a gentle nod, Artan let him go. He needed to hear what the hunters were saying. Maybe they'd tell him something useful. Maybe he'd find out more about the asylum and its location. Straining to hear over the wash of rain, the strong wind slamming into him, he moved several feet closer to the bend.

The hunters' voices echoed from where they'd clearly found shelter. In a cave of some sort, they must have been waiting out the downpour.

"You know what?" one of the hunters said. He had a deep boom to his voice as if he didn't realise just how loud he was. "I think Grandfather Jacks is a lucky man."

The silence suggested the boy walked on thin ice.

"Look at what he does. I mean, who wouldn't want to welcome those two girls from the community into womanhood. Come on, Hawk, surely you've got your eye on that firecracker? She's smoking."

William glanced back. Max stood far enough away to not hear them.

"Although I like the other one," the boy continued. "That

girl has class."

William only realised Artan had drawn closer when he squeezed his left shoulder and tugged him back. But William didn't budge, his pulse quickening, his grip tight on Jezebel's handle.

The loud hunter continued, "What I'd do to be in Grandfather Jacks' shoes. Hey, where are you going?"

Hawk responded to the kid, "I need some space. I suggest you *don't* follow me."

"What's gotten into him?" the boy said.

As Hawk's steps drew closer, William continued to wring Jezebel's handle. He'd take his head off if he came around the bend.

When Artan tugged on his shoulder again, William snapped away from him. This ended now.

"William, we need to get away. We can't fight all of those hunters."

"No, but at least I can take this one down. We'll deal with the others when it comes to it. We can use this narrow path to our advantage."

"This damp and slippery path, you mean? This path they know infinitely better than we do?"

Cyrus had already started to scale the wall with the gentler gradient. The craggy surface gave him places for his feet and hands, offering a similar escape to the one they'd made from the diseased pit.

"Now's not the time, William," Artan said. He slipped the handle of his war hammer down the back of his shirt, freeing his hands for the climb.

"Come on, Hawk," one of the hunters called. "Come back, man. You'll get soaked."

"I need a minute."

Hawk drew closer to the bend, and William held firm for

a second longer. But Cyrus and Artan were right. If he fought them now, they might never get to Matilda and Olga. This would be playing into Grandfather Jacks' hands. Like Artan had done, he slid Jezebel's handle down the back of his sodden shirt before jogging back and joining his friends in their climb out of there.

Cyrus reached the top first, Artan a few seconds later. William finally climbed up, rolling onto the ledge and out of sight. Hawk hadn't yet reached the bend.

Max took up the rear, scrambling up the side of the wall to get away before Hawk appeared. He slipped. William's heart spiked and he gasped.

But Max had only made a small slip from where he struggled to find purchase on the slick walls. The toes of his right boot found another tiny ledge, his fingers turning white from where he gripped on. He felt the wall with his left boot and regained his footing before continuing his climb. Until he slipped again. This time both of his feet went.

William lurched forwards and caught the back of Max's sodden wrists. The rain came down so hard it stung, his clothes clinging to him.

Max desperately tried to find purchase on the wet wall, his feet slipping and sliding. His weight dragged William gradually down with him. Max then froze when one of the hunters called after Hawk for a second time. "Come back. Jack wasn't thinking. You know what he's like."

"I'm fine," Hawk said. In just a few more steps, he'd round the bend. "I just need a moment."

Max slipped by several inches at once, dragging William over the side. Were it not for Artan catching his ankles, they would have both fallen back down to the path. Hawk's steps drew closer. They didn't have time to hide. "Just let us go," William said. "We have no choice but to fight."

CHAPTER 19

Barp!
The sound, accompanied by another sharp blow to the back of her head, roused Olga. The *swish* of her clothes dragged over the stone floor. Two guards pulled her along by her ankles down a long and dark corridor like every corridor she'd travelled in this place. The shadows closed in from all sides, the slight glow from the small suns on the walls ineffective against the swamping darkness.

A throbbing headache pulsed through Olga's eyes. If the rhythmic pain surged any harder, her eyeballs would burst. The rough ground tore into her shoulder blades, but she kept her head raised so she didn't slam it against the stone again. Another two guards dragged Matilda beside her.

Barp!

Olga kicked her feet, both guards gripping on tighter. "Where are you taking us?"

The bright blue glow from one of the poles dazzled her. A guard at her side held it inches from her face. It fizzed and crackled, spitting a restrained fury that craved release.

The guards halted. Olga kicked her legs again, twisting

and turning. The person with the pole moved into the light. Another woman, this one with short black hair. She pulled the pole away, walked close to Olga, gritted her teeth, and pressed the sole of her dirty boot into her neck.

Barp!

Gasping for breath, Olga clamped a grip on the woman's ankle and tried to push her away. But the woman leaned in, pressing incrementally harder, the grit on her boot cutting into Olga's skin.

Stars swam in Olga's vision, and the echo of her ragged pants mocked her struggle. Her heart raced, her world fading. But before she blacked out, a door opened on her right, and the woman lifted her boot. Much like the prison cell, the large wooden door had a small window. Hung on strong steel hinges, it would take a team of people with a battering ram to knock it down.

After dragging her into the cell, the man and woman dropped Olga's feet, her ankles slamming against the ground. The two guards who'd dragged Matilda did the same. Olga stood on wobbly legs, her breathing still tight. The guard who'd crushed her throat close by, Olga kicked the pole from her hands. The long bar spun away from her and clattered into a far wall. The short-haired woman lunged forward, driving a hard blow into Olga's stomach.

Barp!

Olga's diaphragm spasmed and she went down onto one knee. The woman took a two-step run-up, but before she could stick the boot in, several guards caught her and dragged her away. A metallic taste when she coughed, Olga spat blood on the floor.

The two guards who'd dragged Olga along the corridor lifted her by grabbing under her arms. Another two already had Matilda on her feet. The man leaned so close to Olga she smelled his rotten breath, the hot press of his words against her skin. "We own you. You *will* learn to yield."

"I'll die before I do that."

"Careful what you wish for." The guards dragged her over to a line of racks against the far wall.

Barp!

Olga twisted in an attempt to break free. The man kept a hold of her and drove his forehead into her nose, a burst of white light blinding her. When he pulled back, a splash of her blood decorated his forehead.

"Is that all you've got?" Olga said, her eyes watering, blood running over her lips and dripping from her chin.

The man yanked her arm up by her left wrist. He tied it to a bar above her head. The rope he'd used to bind her bit into the cuts already there. The woman on the other side did the same to her other wrist, the same burn of her reopening wounds on that side.

"You think this will stop me?" Olga said, her wrists on fire.

Barp!

The man shoved a cloth into her mouth, his fingers driving it so deep she gagged. He blindfolded her with another strip of fabric, which he tied with a tight knot at the back of her head. "He likes them small and feisty," the man said before gently stroking her face. "I'll make sure I give him my personal recommendation for you."

Olga shook against the bonds at her wrists, her feet now bound at the ankles.

A woman announced, "Praise be to the High Father."

The room responded. At least six guards, the echo of the collective chant swirled around the small and damp dungeon. "Praise be."

The guards left the room and one person entered. The gentle steps of their soft gait, they drew closer to Olga.

Barp!

A sniffing in Olga's ear. The back of her neck clenched. Another sniff sent a spasm twisting along her spine. The man let out a low and aroused groan that melted into words. "Mmmmmmm—I like this one."

Olga snapped forward, but the man caught her brow and shoved her head against the wall. He shook from the force, driving her back against the cold stone, pressing like he wanted to crack her skull. Ten to fifteen seconds passed as he held her in place. A display of his complete control.

Tears streamed from Olga's eyes and she finally yielded.

Grandfather Jacks let her go and stepped back. He laughed, a deep bass note of mirth that came from his toes. "She's feisty. I like the challenge."

A wet tongue ran from the bottom of Olga's chin, up across her lips, and to her nose. The man remained just inches from her. His words shuddered as he pressed into her, his crotch swelling against her thigh. "I love the taste of fresh blood. I like to drink your essence."

Barp!

The echo from the loud tone died out as Grandfather Jacks' gentle steps left the room.

Olga blinked to clear her tears. A swollen lump clogged her throat. A man removed her blindfold and pulled out her gag. Just him alone with them in the cell, he wore a black executioner's hood and long black leather gloves. Other than that, he stood naked from the waist up. Broad shoulders, thick pecs, and a muscly back, he crossed the room to Matilda and removed her blindfold and gag. Her eyes were wide and bloodshot.

The man might have worn a hood, but it didn't hide the

scars around his neck. Similar to Hawk's and Carl's, it looked like someone had tried to decapitate him. What had been done to him? To all three of them?

The glint of a blade at least six inches long in his right hand, the semi-naked man returned to Olga. "You come anywhere near me with that thing," she said, "and I'm going to take it off you and shove it up your arse."

The man halted and tilted his head to one side. His dark eyes glistened as they stared from the depths of his hood.

"You're a really big man, aren't you?" Olga said. "It must take some minerals to be able to dominate bound girls."

The man turned away. Matilda's breaths quickened when he walked over to her, waving his blade in her direction.

Barp!

"What are you doing?" Olga said.

The man swiped his blade through the air and Matilda screamed.

"What are you doing to her?" Olga shook against her bonds, the cuts on her wrists stinging. "Come over here, you coward. Take a piece of me."

Another swipe and Matilda screamed again.

Barp!

"I said come here."

Matilda hung limp and whimpered. Olga fought against her restraints, but they were tied too tight, every tug running a nauseating fiery streak down her forearms. "Fine," she said. "I'll tell you whatever you want to know, just leave her alone."

The man approached Olga with slow and deliberate steps. Blood dripped from the end of his sharp knife. Olga winced in anticipation of his attack.

The man breathed heavily and spoke with a high-pitched lisp. "I think you misunderstand me, little girl. I don't want anything from you. We don't need to *know* anything. The whole purpose of this is to make you pliable enough to receive the High Father's wisdom. And time is of the essence because he would like you compliant for tomorrow night's ceremony."

Barp!

Olga cried when the torturer lifted his blade again. But instead of coming for her, he crossed the room and headed back to Matilda.

CHAPTER 20

William's forearms ached from holding onto Max. It must have been twice as bad for Artan gripping onto his ankles behind him, supporting the weight of both of them. Jezebel's axe head rested against the back of William's skull, daring him to go down and fight. Maybe she had a point. What good did it do anyone hanging there waiting to be taken out with a spear? "Artan," he said, "let us go."

If anything, Artan's grip tightened, and all of them remained frozen as they lay down the slope. In a few more steps, Hawk would appear around the bend.

William shook, his muscles aching. Artan might not let him go, but he couldn't hold Max for much longer.

"Hawk!"

Max turned sharply towards where they expected Hawk to appear. He pulled William a little farther down the slope.

"Will you be long, Hawk?"

The hunter waited for a few seconds before he replied, "No. Come on." His voice grew quieter as he returned to his tribe. "Let's get moving. We have some deer to catch."

About thirty seconds later, Max said, "Can I climb up

now?"

While biting his bottom lip, William breathed through his nose and nodded. Another few useless attempts to find his footing, Max scraped the toes of his boots against the wall before he finally found a small ledge. One toe on it and then the other, his legs shook like William's arms, his entire weight balanced on the very edge of his boots. Another step, a little higher this time. Slower than when he'd been trying to get away in the first place, he made steady progress up the wall.

As if to reassure William, Artan clamped a tighter grip on his ankles. He had him.

Max climbed over William, grabbing the sides of his body first. He reached over his back and grabbed his belt. He gripped the fabric of his trousers on the back of his thighs before moving up to Artan as he continued his climb.

Artan tugged William's ankles, pulling him up the wall. Although William tried to help by pushing off the hard steel, the others worked together, moving him quicker than he could keep up, his stomach scraping as they pulled him clear.

The others moved on as William took the time to shake his arms in an attempt to encourage the life back into them. But it would take longer than a few seconds for the fatigue to ease. Even Jezebel's weight had become a burden.

William joined Cyrus and the others. They stood on a ledge overlooking the hunters. They were gathered around the mouth of the cave they'd used to seek shelter from the rain. Close to twenty fit boys and young men, if they'd been drawn into combat, they would have wiped the floor with William and his friends.

The group of hunters waited for the broad-shouldered Hawk to pass them. He moved with heavy steps and a wide strut unique to someone with thighs as thick as his.

Although the hunters had gathered around idly waiting, when Hawk got to the front, they fell into single file, raised their spears, and followed their leader. They might not have looked like it seconds before, but now they were on the move, this lot were ready to fight.

The wind even stronger now they were higher up, it hammered against William, who stepped back from the edge.

"Do you think the girls have given up on us?" Max said once they'd all pulled back. "From what those hunters were just saying about Grandfather Jacks, they have a lot of other things to deal with."

"I'm not sure it matters whether they're thinking about us or not," Cyrus said. He reached across and clapped a hand on Max's sodden shoulder. Max shrugged it off and pulled away from him, but Cyrus continued anyway. "We're going to find them and get them away from that man and his community before it's too late. And don't worry about Olga. Not only can she look after herself, but she will have worked out by now why you pushed her away. I'm sure she's had plenty of time to think."

"Maybe you should keep your thoughts to yourself," Max said. "How about you focus on what you can do to help us in this moment rather than speculating on my relationships?"

Had William had more to offer, he would have said it, but Cyrus was right and Max was angry. He wouldn't calm down until they found Olga. They did need to keep moving, and to some extent it didn't matter what the girls thought. Or what the boys thought they thought. After all, they could only guess what went through the girls' minds at that moment. And the fact remained, they had to get to the community before the full moon. As long as they did that, they stood a chance of getting them away from there. He flicked his head in the direction they needed to go. "Come on, let's keep moving. If we stay away from the edge, the hunters won't see us up here."

From a distance, the top of the wall had looked flat, but now they were on it, it had as many hills and valleys as any other terrain. Although William had encouraged them to move on, he allowed the others to go ahead of him, taking up the rear while Artan led.

Many of the birds in the sky above them were new to William. Some of them were larger than he'd thought possible. In Edin, he'd seen robins, crows, and pigeons. Once or twice a month, a sparrowhawk would streak through the sky, but they never stopped long enough to allow him a good look. The wingspans of some of the birds now overhead stretched at least a metre wide. They showed off their impressive silhouettes while riding the currents, some of them flapping to remain still as they hovered. They watched the ground, ready to dive.

Artan stopped, but William couldn't see why until he caught up to him and recognised the man. "He's one of the retired hunters." All four of them gathered around the corpse in their path. "I recognise him from Umbriel. Although I can't remember his name. I want to say Carl. He was a miserable bastard."

"Weren't they all?" Artan said.

"You think he was one of the hunters who took the girls?" Max said.

Artan shrugged. "His wounds are fresh."

One of the larger birds hovered above them. William gripped Jezebel tighter. No matter how magnificent the creature, if that sharp beak and talons dived on them right now, he'd have no problem swinging for it.

Cyrus said, "But who did *that* to him? I don't believe this has anything to do with the girls."

The corpse had a swollen and bloody face from where he'd clearly been beaten to death or very close to it. Grim, but maybe necessary in a fight. But the cuts on his eyes ... they were something else. Two deep crosses as if whoever attacked him wanted to make sure he'd never see again. Or maybe to prevent him from witnessing what they were about to do to him. The gashes were at least an inch long. They were so deep, flashes of white bone glistened in the crimson.

The man's shirt had been ripped open. A strong body, but flabby with age, the word *sinner* had been scored across his fleshy chest. As with the cuts on his eyes, they ran deep enough to reveal glimpses of the bone beneath.

"And whoever did that to him," William said, "what does it mean for the girls?"

Several snapping heaves took over Cyrus, who walked away from the corpse. Artan and Max followed a few seconds later, Max shaking his head at Cyrus' weak stomach. About six feet away, Artan halted. "Come on, William. There's nothing more to see here."

But what did it mean for the girls? Could they have done this? Matilda, no, but maybe Olga. Rage could do strange things to people. And if she had done it to him, what had the man done to her to warrant such an extreme response?

"Artan!" Cyrus had now walked at least twenty feet away from the others. He pointed down. "There's a hole. It might be a way out of here."

After staring at the bloody crosses for a second or two longer, William moved off to be with his friends. Where were the girls right now, and what had happened to them since leaving Umbriel?

The others stood over a square tunnel cut into the steel, the angle kinder than the wall they'd scaled to get away from Hawk. "Matilda could climb down that in a heartbeat."

"I'll do it," Cyrus said. "I can get down there and back out again if I need to."

"Are you sure?" Artan said.

"I reckon it's a way out of here. We need to be going lower if we stand any chance of getting off this damn wall. With how sheer the front of it was, I'm guessing the back's as bad."

"And you're sure you want to climb down there?" Max said.

"Climbing's one of the things I *can* do," Cyrus said.

Artan patted his friend on the back. "I think you're right, one of us should go down and check it out. If you need me, shout."

Cyrus dropped down and sat on the edge of the square hole, hanging his feet into the chute. He turned one hundred and eighty degrees and dropped his entire body down, gripping onto the lip of the hole as he lowered himself. His arms at full stretch, he paused for no more than half a second before he let go, sliding backwards into what would hopefully turn out to be their exit.

Although they'd watched Cyrus to the end of the chute, they lost sight of him when he went exploring. About a minute later, he reappeared at the bottom of the hole. His voice echoed in the tunnel. "It's a way out. Come on."

"It's safe?" Max said.

"Yeah, it's fine."

Artan, as always, put more trust in Cyrus than the rest of them, slipping his war hammer down the back of his shirt and sliding down the long chute to be with his friend. William followed next, a jolt snapping through his body when his feet hit the unforgiving ground. He stood aside for Max.

A tunnel led from the bottom of the chute. Although a steep decline, they could still walk it.

William followed the others around a bend and into the dazzling daylight. A small cave opened up. Ten feet square, it overlooked grassy wastelands much like those they'd left behind. Although here, instead of rocks and rubble littering the landscape, large chunks of steel sat amongst the grass. Maybe left over from building the wall. It had been turned into a waste product here. Darkness masked the route they'd taken. From where William now stood, he couldn't see the tunnel he'd just emerged from.

A slight glint to his right, William's heart flipped, his hand shaking when he picked it up.

"What is it?" Cyrus said.

Artan rubbed William's back and spoke with a sigh. "It's Matilda's hair clip."

A lump swelled in William's throat. He coughed to clear it. "It was my mum's." He turned the small metal hummingbird over in his shaking hands. "She gave it to her when we went on national service." His eyes burned. Fatigue and grief choked him again and he gulped so he could get his words out. "It seems like such a long time ago now."

In the silence of the cave, William forced a laugh. "My god, listen to me. At least this tells us the girls made it farther than that corpse up there. Maybe they got away from their captors."

"Maybe they *were* the ones who did that to him?" Max said.

"At least at this point, they were still alive," Cyrus said. "We'll find them."

Artan pointed out into the wastelands. "So we wait here until we see those hunters move on, and then we go find Grandfather Jacks' community? We're only half a day's walk away. We have the time to wait it out."

"And we stand no chance against a pack of hunters with

spears in the open," Cyrus said. "There are too many of them."

Max tutted. "Of course you'd say that. You're a coward."

"I think he's right," Artan said. "What kind of fool would take on the odds of us against them?"

The muscles in Max's jaw bulged when he clenched it.

A throbbing buzz of fatigue ran through William. Last night's sleep beneath a blanket of corpses hadn't been the most restful experience. He dropped down onto the cold metal ground, cross-legged as he faced out into the wild lands. He lifted one side of his bottom to pull the map from his back pocket.

The other boys gathered around. William pointed at the map. "This is where we need to get to. I know we have a day and a half, but we don't know what this side of the wall's like. The sooner the hunters get clear, the better. I'd rather get to Grandfather Jacks' community with time to spare."

It took no more than five minutes for the first of the hunters to step into view. Hawk continued to lead the line. They probably couldn't see them in the shadowy cave, but William shifted back to be certain, and the others followed him.

More and more of the hunters walked into the long grass before Cyrus said, "That's nineteen. That's all of them."

"You counted them when we were back on the wall?" Max said. It sounded like an accusation, his fury driving his words.

Cyrus shrugged. "I thought it would be useful to know."

Artan smiled.

William nodded at the boy. He might not be much of a fighter, but he had other skills. "Well done, Cyrus. I'm glad someone was thinking. So now we know they're all out, we just need to wait long enough for them to get far away."

CHAPTER 21

Barp! The noise rattled Olga's bones. When she'd seen Dianna twitch at the alarm, it gave her an insight into her own future. Her reaction had grown worse, the deep single note bouncing around inside her skull every time it sounded. The squeaky wheel on her trolley had a subtler effect but no less penetrative. It bored into her psyche as she wobbled along the stone corridor, upright on the trolley and tilted back to allow the guard to push.

Crack! Someone opened a lock somewhere. Blindfolded and gagged again, they'd strapped Olga to her metal trolley with leather belts. They were much like the ones they'd pinned her to the stretcher with when they'd brought her and Matilda to this vile place. Hinges groaned and an outside breeze whooshed in, driving away the reek of damp.

Olga's trolley moved on, the squeak of another set of wheels close by. It had to be Matilda. Soon after the torturer had let Olga watch him attack her friend, he'd blindfolded and gagged both of them again. Suspended by ropes in the darkness, she'd listened to Matilda whimper.

Outside and in the full force of the wind, the shriek of

diseased came close. They must have been in the gothic steel tunnel they'd travelled down when entering the asylum.

Barp! The noise carried across the landscape. Although it was quieter now they were outside and around the back of the building. Dianna had said the sound called the diseased to the front. How many were gathered there at this moment?

Something slammed into the steel fence on Olga's left. Adrenaline drove her pulse, but she didn't have the range of movement to flinch. Hopefully the guards pushing her had the good sense to avoid danger.

Barp! The tone had grown much more distant now and got drowned out by the wails and screams of the diseased.

The gag leeched the moisture from Olga's mouth. Her throat arid, it clamped with a permanent half-heave. Her tongue ached from where she pushed against the dry cloth, trying to force it out.

Crack! Another freeing bolt followed by more groaning hinges from a gate being opened.

They passed through another door a few minutes later and entered a new building. Light flooded into Olga's world when the guard behind her removed her blindfold. Had she not been gagged, she would have gasped. It took a few seconds for the bright corridor to come into focus. A glass ceiling let in more daylight than she'd seen in hours. The glare reflected off the pure white walls. Even on a day as overcast as this, the sun lit the corridor as if they were being led on their final journey to heaven. Or to the High Father?

Two large metal doors at the end of the corridor, they parted when Olga got close. They welcomed them into a large open room. It too had a glass ceiling.

They pushed Olga up an aisle, pews on either side. The back wall had a vibrant mural depicting the silhouette of a tall man in a leather outback hat. His features were hidden by the brilliant glow from behind him, the light of the High Father. Stretched out before him lay a sea of prostrate women, teenage girls, and children. Hard to tell, but it looked like the children were mostly boys.

Once they'd gotten to the end of the aisle, they turned Olga ninety degrees to the right. The guard wheeling Matilda brought her forwards and turned the trolley so they faced one another. The woman pushing Matilda pulled the cloth from her mouth and walked back down the aisle. The one who'd pushed Olga did the same for her before she also left.

A large white bandage wrapped Matilda's left thigh. Blood seeped through it. The large stain stretched about four inches wide and glistened. "I'm so sorry," Olga said.

"Why are you sorry? You didn't do it."

"No, but he did it because of me."

"They'll use whatever they can against us in this place. Besides, he cut me, and it hurt, but I think there's only so far they'll go. Despite the blood, it's only surface damage. I can't see Grandfather Jacks approving people hurting his brides." When Olga clenched her jaw, Matilda added, "I'm telling you I'm okay, so I need you to keep a lid on your rage."

"But I won't let Grandfather Jacks do this."

"I don't intend to either, but please save your fight for when it counts."

The automatic doors they'd come through opened again. Two girls walked in. Heidi and the girl with mousy-brown hair, her right foot still limp and dragging as she hobbled up the aisle.

"You were saying they'll only go so far …" Olga said.

Heidi passed through the gap between Olga and Matilda. She pulled a tight-lipped smile before walking up to the altar. She stood in one of five circles marked on the ground. The girl with the broken ankle stood in another one.

An older woman with grey hair and a tape measure around her neck whisked into the room. Frantic like a small bird, her shrill voice rang out in the large space. "This is a wedding rehearsal. We need to make sure we're all ready and know what we're doing for tomorrow evening. I've promised Grandfather Jacks it will be the best one yet. He's so excited. He's promised to attend today to see if he can assist in any way." The woman almost sang the last bit, a neurotic smile, her face streaked with worry lines, "so it's best behaviour, ladies."

"Fuck that!" Olga muttered. Matilda pinned her with a hard stare.

"You two." The wedding organiser pointed at Olga and Matilda. "You'd do well to learn from these girls here. This is what Grandfather Jacks needs from his brides."

"Docile compliance?" Olga said. This time she avoided Matilda's eye.

The brown-haired girl smiled, oblivious to anything but her devotion to Grandfather Jacks. Her glassy and unblinking eyes streamed tears of joy as she stared into the middle distance. Heidi had turned several shades paler.

A deep whir shook the ground. The vibrations ran up through the wheels of Olga's trolley. "What's going on?"

Circular cages rose through the floor, trapping the two girls who'd stood in the rings surrounding the altar. Three more cages entrapped the empty circles next to the girls, and a platform rose from the floor in the centre. The three empty cages must have been intended for Olga, Matilda, and Dianna. The platform was clearly for Grandfather Jacks.

The cages clicked into place, and silence filled the large room before Olga finally said, "Hell no!"

The wedding organiser gasped. The refusal or use of the word *hell*? Hard to tell. But Olga stood by both of them.

"No way am I going in that cage."

"*Olga!*" Matilda said.

"Shh!" The avian woman flapped her arms as if they were on fire. She walked in circles. "Shh! He'll be here soon."

"Good," Olga said. "I'll tell him to go to hell to his face."

"It's no good," the woman said, her shrill voice swirling around the room. "It's no good. Take them away. Take them away now."

Four guards entered the room and ran up the aisle. Two went to the back of Olga's trolley, two to Matilda's. They turned Olga around and led her away at a jog, the metal wheels of her steel cart clacking as they ran over the uneven surface.

"Give them some time to reflect," the wedding organiser called after them. "Let them rest in a room with beds in, untie them, and feed them. They need to be in a better frame of mind for tomorrow night."

"See," Olga called back to Matilda, raising her voice to be heard over their clattering exit. "Sometimes the best thing you can do is tell someone to go fuck themselves."

CHAPTER 22

Were it up to William, they would have moved off ten minutes after the hunters left. But it made sense to wait. To allow the group of boys to get far away. Who knew where the next good hiding spot would be, and the last thing they needed was to be caught out in the middle of the wild lands against experienced hunters with spears. The choice made sense, but he didn't have to like it. At all.

William swung his legs, letting them hang down from the mouth of the cave, slapping his heels against the hard steel wall. The long grass in the meadow bent and swayed at the weather's whim. The hummingbird hair clip in his right hand, he turned it over, blinking against the sting in his eyes. There had been so many times where he'd been somewhere high, on the roof of a building or a tall wall in Edin, Matilda beside him as they spent hours planning a future that would never come. But he wouldn't give up on her. They'd be within their rights to think the boys hadn't made it, but as long as there was a chance Matilda and Olga were still alive, he wouldn't ever give up.

William shot backwards, his legs flipping up into the air

when Artan pulled him into the shadows. He twisted free from the boy. "What the hell are you doing?"

Artan pressed a finger to his lips before pointing out into the meadow.

Thank god Artan had seen them. A group of men and women. Hard to identify which were which from this distance. All of them had long and scraggly hair. Dreadlocked, wild, they all wore animal furs, many of them just vests and trousers, a patchwork of colours from black fur, to the white of rabbit's tails.

"Do you think they have anything to do with the hunters?" Max said.

Artan shook his head. "No."

William raised an eyebrow. "You seem quite certain."

"Some of them have swords."

It made sense. The hunters had tossed away William's and his friends' swords the second they'd encountered them.

"Do you think we should ask for their help?" Cyrus said.

William shook his head. "I think the fewer people we talk to or mix with, the better. Especially until we find the girls. I'm not ready to trust anyone at the moment."

His back now against the cold steel wall with the others, William remained in the shadows. They were hidden from view, yet the crew of people, twenty-three of them in total—or at least twenty-three he could see—headed straight for them. Cyrus had been sensible to count the hunters. William's stomach sank. "I think they must have seen me before you pulled me back, Artan."

One solitary word, it bounced off the solid walls and died. "Yep." He then added, "Maybe we should take some control and ask them for help?"

"Or we go back the way we came?" Max said.

William's heart quickened and he held on to his initial

response. They were a team and had to make a decision as one. The hummingbird clip still in his hand, he said, "I'm more keen to go towards the girls. I know we still have some time before the full moon, but we could lose that time with a bad decision."

"Well, they're getting closer," Artan said, "so whatever choice we make, we need to make it soon. Who says we go back?"

Max raised his hand, his face reddening at the attention from his friends.

"And who says we go to those people?"

Cyrus and William raised their hands. A second later, Artan copied them and said, "They've seen us now, so instead of running, I think we should try to find a way to move forwards."

William took the lead. "Let's do this." Shifting to the edge of the cave, he tossed Jezebel out into the long and damp grass, pocketed the intricate hair clip, and turned around so he faced his friends, showing the approaching tribe his back. He then hung down from the ledge, his legs swinging. A drop of about five feet remained. He let go and fell.

As Cyrus, Artan, and then Max followed him, William retrieved Jezebel and stepped away from the edge of the wall. His foot turned slightly when he stood on something hard. A knife, a hunter's knife like the ones they'd seen in Umbriel. He turned it over in his grip, the long blade catching the light. Had one of the pack they'd been following dropped it? Had the girls swiped it from their captors? Had it been the blade that inflicted the damage on the corpse they found? William handed the knife to Artan.

"What's this for?"

"You're the one who makes spears. I figured this might be of use to you."

One spear and one knife. Now armed like a hunter, Artan handed his war hammer to Max.

The frown that had become synonymous with Max softened. "You sure?"

Artan nodded.

As the group drew closer, Max spoke from the side of his mouth. "I know it goes without saying, but I want to avoid showing these people what I can do unless I have to."

"Of course," William said, the other two nodding their agreement.

The large group presented a more intimidating prospect now they were on the ground with them. They spread out like a net widening to catch prey. All of them had their spears raised. Maybe the hunters had been wise to be so beholden to their primary weapon. Not only did this crowd outnumber them, but they could take them down from a distance. They were in control. If William could have returned to the cave and taken Max's option now, he would. But they were too late to change their minds. Hopefully that decision hadn't just ended their lives.

CHAPTER 23

"Of course the door's locked," Olga said, letting go of the large steel handle. The door similar to the cell they'd shared with Dianna, Heidi, and the broken mousy-brown haired girl. Although the similarities ended there. "But at least we have comfort now." The bed sank when Olga sat on it, the white sheets freshly cleaned. A floor of stone like everywhere else in the asylum, but at least it had been swept. At least the place didn't stink of sweat and piss. "Sometimes kicking off gets you what you need. Maybe they're trying a different approach. Maybe they recognise with time running out, the ceremony being tomorrow night, that being nice might get them somewhere."

Barp!

"You're not convinced?" Olga said to the frowning Matilda.

Matilda lay on one of the beds and stared up at the ceiling. "I think Heidi and the other girl should be a lesson to us."

"That we need to be like them?"

"Maybe. They're *ready* for Grandfather Jacks, after all."

"You saying we should pretend?"

"Maybe."

"No." Olga paced the small yet clean room. "That isn't me. I'd rather die than give in like those two girls have."

Barp!

"You might have to." Although Olga opened her mouth to reply, Matilda cut her off. "Anyway, my main aim is to get away from this place as soon as possible and find William, Artan, and the others."

"Well, at least we're agreed on that."

A loud knock at the door, the silhouette of someone peering in through the small barred window. There were more small glass suns in this room than anywhere they'd been so far. They cast a warm, almost welcoming glow. The person in the hallway stood far enough back for the shadows to hide their features.

Crack! The hinges groaned as the door opened. Olga twisted her feet where she stood and balled her fists. The crackle of one of the blue poles loosed some of the tension in her frame and she stepped back a pace.

Barp!

"You!" One of the guards, a short and wide man with a shaved head and scars around his neck like Hawk and Carl, pointed at Matilda. His stick crackled and buzzed with the blue glow. "Move. Get over against that far wall." He turned on Olga, his eyes hidden in the shadow cast by his thick brow. "You get over there too."

Olga swallowed a dry gulp and moved to stand beside Matilda, the stone wall cold against her back. Maybe she'd grown too confident about their situation too soon?

Another man entered the room. He had a plate in each hand. He walked with his head bowed, his bottom lip protruding as he addressed the ground. "Here's your dinner.

Deer, potatoes, and carrots. The High Father wanted you to know it's what he's eating right now."

Barp!

"See," Olga said from the side of her mouth. "They are trying a different approach."

The man with the plates placed one on Olga's bed. "He said he's a patient man. He'd love to marry you on this cycle, but he's a patient man." After he'd placed the second plate on Matilda's bed, he left the room. He continued to avoid eye contact. The guard with the blue pole waved it in their direction before he too exited. On his way out, he slammed the door and cracked the bolt shut.

Matilda had been pale before the men had entered the room. If anything, her skin had now turned translucent. "What's wrong?" Olga said. "We've been fed. We have comfort. Surely this is a better situation to break out from?"

"Did you hear what he just said? About the cycles. About patience."

Too confident in her own actions, Olga hadn't joined the dots. "Oh shit!"

"Exactly," Matilda said. "There's a full moon once a month. If we're not ready this month, he's patient enough to wait."

CHAPTER 24

A man and a woman separated from the group and continued towards the boys. The rest of the pack formed a semicircle, closing in to cut off any chance of escape. Spears in one hand, weapons—from blades to clubs to axes—in the other, each of them came ready for war. It started with a clicking sound, one of them snapping their teeth together. The rest joined in, the clicks rising in frequency until the clacking teeth turned into a continuous tone. Some of them hummed a deep bass note. The nerve-rattling sound made the wall of warriors utterly impenetrable.

The two who had broken away from the group edged slowly closer. The woman stood no more than five feet six inches tall, and she had a slight yet lithe frame. Blonde hair, pale skin, and a large gap between her front teeth, which she had no problem displaying in a wide grin. The man beside her stood as tall as William. Dark skin, not quite as dark as William's, but several shades deeper than Artan's. Were his long black hair not matted and tied with bones and sticks, it would have hung dead straight. His ochre eyes penetrated them as if he searched the boys for their lies before they'd left their mouths.

"Hi," the woman said, her tone as chipper as her demeanour. It stood in stark contrast to the humming and clicking warriors at her back.

Cyrus stepped forwards and offered his hand, his voice wavering. "Hi. I'm Cyrus."

Too late to drag him back now, William kept his mouth shut while Cyrus shook hands with the two leaders.

"This is Artan, William, and Max," Cyrus said.

The man spoke this time. "We need you to lower your weapons."

Max shook his head and pulled his war hammer close to his chest. "Ain't no way I'm giving this up."

"We're not asking you to give it up," the woman said, "just lower it. You're all standing like you're ready for war. I find it—" she looked up as if searching for the word, her smile returning when she said "—disconcerting."

The boys looked at one another before Artan led them in lowering both his spear and knife.

"Thank you," the man said. "My name's Serj and this is Collette."

"We're nomads," Collette said. "We have no home, so we live in the wild lands. We like the freedom. We hunt; we move around; we stay wherever takes our fancy."

Cyrus shrugged. "We have no home now either."

"You wanna give them our whole life story?" William said.

Collette, who seemed the true leader of the two, acknowledged William with a nod. "I understand. You don't know us; you shouldn't be too trusting. It's a hard world out here. Especially south of the funnel. You're northerners?"

The way she said it turned through William, twisting his back. Utter disdain for those north of the funnel. "We're from the north, yes."

"Lucky you," she said. "We could tell. You have the marks of someone who hasn't had too much cause to hide. Who doesn't know the struggles of the south."

"What do you know of our struggles?" William stepped forward and Artan pulled him back. The hunters in the semi-circle all raised their weapons. Their hum grew louder; their teeth clicked harder.

"Look," Serj said, "we're not bad people, and we're not here to fight you."

"What are you here for, then?" Max said.

"We figured you might want some help. We saw you"—he pointed at William—"from a mile away. You sat on the edge of the wall like a tourist."

Heat flushed William's cheeks.

"We thought we'd get to you first. Come say hi; maybe offer a few words of advice."

"And there's nothing better than unsolicited advice," William said.

Collette raised her thin eyebrows. "Especially when it saves your life, eh?"

William bit back his response.

"Please," Serj said, "take the advice with the goodwill that's intended. You won't last long on this side of the funnel if you don't learn the ways of the people here. Can you hunt?"

"We have to be somewhere," William said.

"First, you hunt," Collette said as she leaned the tip of her spear in William's direction.

The semicircle tightened again, the nomads clicking and

humming even louder than before. They offered spears to the boys.

After a slight hesitation, William and the others took the spears. At least they still had nearly a day and a half until the full moon.

CHAPTER 25

"What do you think the boys are doing right now?" Olga said.

Matilda sighed and paused as she stared into space with the hint of a tearful glaze covering her brown eyes. She filled her lungs and turned her attention to Olga. "What you and I would be doing."

"You think they're trying to track us down?"

"Absolutely."

"And you think they're close?"

"Who knows?" Matilda lost focus again. "Although, what I do know is we need to find a way out of here on our own."

"Damn straight," Olga said. "It's just how."

"Exactly."

Crack! The lock opened. A reminder that while they might have been staying in a more luxurious room, they were still prisoners. A tall blonde woman with a mean scowl entered. Taller than both Olga and Matilda, she had short hair and harsh wrinkles around her eyes, which were accentuated by the brown lines of dirt filling them. She had red blotches all over her skin, and several of her teeth were missing.

Olga tutted and shook her head. "What is it with you lot? How can you do this man's bidding? Surely you can see it's all a ruse so he can bed young girls?"

The woman wore tatty boots with hard soles, the clip of them against the stone floor as she marched over to Olga. Although Olga winced, the woman stopped just inches from her, the wrinkles around her eyes deepening. "You've had your rest now. You've been fed. We were going to leave you until next month, but Grandfather Jacks has received a message from the High Father that we should try one last time."

"Don't you mean the dirty old man has a hard-on for either me or Matilda, and he doesn't want to wait?"

Thwack! The woman caught Olga with a backhand, knocking her to the ground.

Her ears ringing, her face throbbing from the blow, Olga stood up on wobbly legs, clamped her jaw, and raised her chin. Her view of Grandfather Jacks' dirty guard blurred because of her watering eyes.

The blonde woman drew a slow intake of breath through her wide nose, her large bosom lifting as she filled her lungs. She swiped her fringe from her brow with one thick sausage finger. "Now, while *I* don't think you can be helped, I'm willing to listen to the High Father to see if there is a way to get you both ready for tomorrow night."

"We're ready," Matilda said.

Olga gasped. After she'd stood up to this woman's bullshit, Matilda had now sold them both out. Why didn't she go and jump into Grandfather Jacks' bed right now? They might have discussed it, but she hadn't agreed. She would not marry the man, regardless of what Matilda did.

Heat radiated from Olga's cheek, but she kept her arms at her sides and resisted the urge to rub it. Matilda could do what she wanted, but she wouldn't show this woman she'd gotten to her. She wouldn't yield. Ever.

The tall blonde woman leaned so close to Olga their noses touched. Her greasy skin carried a stench of old dirt. When she spoke, her words rode on a wave of halitosis. "This one doesn't look ready."

The cuts on Matilda's thigh kept Olga's mouth shut. She couldn't be responsible for them torturing her again.

The blonde woman sniffed Olga. "She doesn't smell ready either. I'm not convinced." The woman pulled back and her tone lightened. "But I need to try. I promised the High Father I'd do all I could to get you both ready. We have a lot of work to do in a very short time. We need to make sure we have you in the purest state possible for the ceremony. You need to come free of baggage. Relieved of your anger. This is for your own good. We have to help you on your path to enlightenment. Otherwise, what other reason is there for us being alive?"

"That's what he calls it, is it?" Olga said.

The blonde woman let out a low growl. "We're here to serve."

"How does taking advantage of little girls serve anyone? How young are some of them? Twelve? Thirteen?"

The right side of Olga's face lit up again and she stumbled from the woman's next blow, her ears ringing with a higher pitch than before. At least she'd attacked her and not Matilda. A deep ache nestled in her jaw, but as much as she wanted to open and close it to work away some of the pain, she bit down harder and rode out the harsh sting.

The *fizz* of the blue poles sounded outside in the corridor. Their bright glow entered ahead of the two guards carrying them. Two men, they each had a female guard behind them who wheeled in a metal trolley. The leather straps hung down, ready to pin Olga and Matilda in place.

Matilda walked over to one of the trolleys, and Olga's jaw fell loose. Her face alive with the buzzing sting of the woman's attack, she frowned but kept her thoughts to herself. Matilda could do whatever she wanted, but that didn't mean Olga had to take this bullshit. She sat down on her bed.

One of the guards with the fizzing blue pole jabbed Matilda's thigh on the bandage, dropping her to the cold stone floor before sending her body flipping with a prolonged press against her back.

"All right!" Olga said, barging the tall blonde woman aside as she walked to the other trolley. "Jesus."

The man jabbed Matilda on the back of her right arm, the limb snapping away from her. The guard spoke through clenched teeth. "The High Father *not* Jesus."

Even after the attack, Matilda's brown eyes remained calm. She nodded at Olga. The silent gesture asked her if she was okay. How could she be concerned for Olga in this moment?

The bars of the metal trolley against her back, the smell of leather when the woman strapped Olga's head in place before pinning her arms to her sides.

Barp! The sound shuddered through the building like a deep barking cough. It had gone on the entire time, but it rang louder through the long dark corridors. The small suns lined the walls. The woman pushing Olga's trolley let Matilda's guard go ahead of them.

They turned right and then another immediate right, the path dropping down at a steep angle. The hallways had been lined with glass suns, but this plunge into the depths of the asylum had none. Inky blackness, they were descending into hell. The rock in Olga's stomach tightened. How could things get worse than they were now?

Barp! The only measure of time in this place. Several more deep tones shook the old building as they plunged deeper and deeper, Olga's trolley wobbling with its wonky wheel, the squeak of it echoing in the dark and cramped space.

Crack! Another large wooden door. Another old lock. The groaning of another set of hinges, Matilda vanished into the shadows inside, disappearing from sight before they pushed Olga in after her.

Barp!

Colder than any other part of the asylum, the damp clung to Olga's skin the second she entered the room. A funky reek of mould, it plugged her nostrils.

The room then lit up so bright it blinded Olga. The strap across her brow prevented her from turning away from the glare. She squinted and it took several seconds for her to regain her sight. The blonde woman stood over to one side by a white switch. A glass sun hung from the ceiling. Larger than any she'd seen before. Even larger than the one in the barn in Umbriel. It glowed pure white.

The walls and floor of the cell glistened, reflecting the light. They put plastic muffs over Matilda's ears. Although Matilda kept her eyes on Olga, she also kept her mouth shut. They didn't need to be getting themselves into any more trouble.

The blonde woman flicked a switch on the side of Matilda's muffs, and Matilda's eyes narrowed with her hard frown. What were they doing to her?

A pair of muffs for Olga, the blonde woman breathed heavily as she slipped them over her ears. They were cushioned on the part resting against Olga's head. They were a snug fit. A slight click from where the woman flicked the switch on the right side.

Assaulted by crying babies, Olga dragged in a sharp breath. They screamed as if being tortured, whining and yelling, the high-pitched wails driving nails into her ears. She shouted but couldn't even hear her own voice. "What the hell is this? What are you doing? Turn it off. Turn it off."

The cries grew louder, cutting to Olga's core.

Then they stopped.

The muscles in Olga's body loosened. Until …

His deep rasping voice. The same voice she'd heard when blindfolded in the other room. The voice of Grandfather Jacks, the man who'd licked the blood from her face. Was he in the room with them now? "Praise be to the High Father. I accept the High Father into my life. Everything I do is in servitude to the High Father. I love the High Father. I'm one with the High Father."

Silence.

Then quietly, in the distance, the cries started again as if the babies were several rooms away. They grew louder and louder, screaming, wailing. Distressed infants, they needed help. They grew so loud Olga's ears rang. Yet, all the while, as Olga twisted and turned, the sounds churning through her, Matilda remained straight-faced. Even the frown she'd worn into the room had lifted.

The first to leave were the two women who'd steered the trolleys. The men with the poles next. The blonde woman leaned close to Olga, her stare flicking left and right as she looked from one of Olga's eyes to the other. She pulled a tight-lipped smile before she also left.

The screams tearing through her skull, Olga tried to focus on Matilda's calm. To find a shred of it to hang onto.

The bright sun blinked off and back on again.

It snapped Olga from the torment.

It did it again, breaking Olga's focus a second time.

Then again.

Each time the gaps grew shorter, the blinking on and off, on and off. The screams grew louder. The blinking came quicker. On, off. On, off. On, off.

Milliseconds between each blink, the strobe grew faster and faster, each burst of light stabbing into Olga's brain. Every scream cut to her core.

All the while, Matilda remained resolute.

The salty taste of her own tears, Olga opened and closed her mouth, but for the first time in as long as she could remember, she had no words.

CHAPTER 26

An order masquerading as a question: can you hunt? It very quickly turned into *first we hunt*. Outnumbered by the nomads, they were their prisoners for now. But at least they still had over a day until the full moon.

William chewed on a piece of cooked meat, the fire in front of him hissing, popping, and spitting as the wood burned and animal fat dropped into the flames. They were eating one of the three deer caught by Artan. Twenty-seven of them had gone out hunting, and Artan had been the only one to make multiple kills. Two hours had passed since they'd met the nomads at the bottom of the large wall. At least their stomachs were full, but anxiety gnawed away at William. They needed to move on. Had he been given the choice, he would have rather remained hungry and gone after the girls.

The knife they'd found on the ground in his right hand, a stick in his left, Artan chewed on deer meat while whittling another spear.

"You're quite the hunter," Collette said. Although she delivered a compliment, her words were spiked, her face taut.

Almost an accusation. It turned into a demand. "We could use someone like you."

If Artan could have ignored her, he probably would have. Instead, he did the bare minimum, lifting his head ever so slightly in acknowledgement that she'd spoken to him before he continued to work on his spear, making eye contact with William for the briefest moment.

William knew Matilda's brother well enough. They were on the same page. They needed to get away from these people as soon as they could. It helped that they agreed, but if they hadn't, he'd learned to trust Artan's intuition over his own.

"We'd like to give you this." Serj held a fur waistcoat in Artan's direction.

Again, Artan slightly tilted his head but nothing more. William took the coat and laid it by his friend.

"It's a tough world south of the funnel," Collette said. They were sat in the open plains, the fire shielded from the wind by a large steel rock. At least half the nomads had remained on their feet, their spears raised as they stood guard. Were they trying to keep William and his friends from leaving, or trying to protect them?

"Although," Collette added, "I reckon with Artan on your side, you might do all right."

"Why's it so much harder in the south?" William said.

Collette shook her head. "This ain't *the* south, just south of the funnel. Although, I suppose, when you're from the other side, everything's south, right?"

William shrugged.

"It's just harder," Serj said, his beard glistening with deer grease. "You lot from the north don't know what it is to struggle."

"Our city fell," Max said. The frown he'd worn since Umbriel remained. "Thousands of people were turned overnight. A city with years of history, devastated by the diseased. Have you ever seen that many diseased in one place?"

A woman sat on Collette's left. The only one of the group with a bald head, she had rolls of fat around her neck. She snorted a laugh. "Have you ever heard of a swarm?"

"What's a swarm?" Cyrus said.

"I'll take that as a no," the bald woman said, her green eyes widening as she stared into the middle distance. "They start at around ten thousand strong. Some of them contain hundreds of thousands of the things." She chewed with her mouth open. "They're a plague that destroys everything in their path."

"If it's so tough down here, why don't you go north of the funnel?" William said.

"Some people do." Serj bit a large chunk of meat from a bone. "But we plan to head south one of these days. *Farther* south. South of the wall."

Even Artan paused his whittling to look at Serj.

"What's south of the wall?" Cyrus said.

Collette took over. "No one knows for sure. But they say life's easier there. Like *much* easier. There's more luxury than we've ever known. There are no diseased. Food's readily available. As is water … shelter …"

"So why haven't you gone?"

"If only it were that easy," Serj said. "They say the journey to even get to the wall is one fraught with so many dangers that to take it is to invite madness. We've seen some who have tried to go, but have fallen short. They may return physically, but they've left their minds at the wall. Duncan's one of them."

A man with long ginger hair and a swinging jaw, he had pale skin and glazed eyes. Despite the meat on offer from a successful hunt, he chewed on a bone like a dog, gnawing the marrow inside.

"So what makes you think you can do any better than he did?" Artan said.

"Honestly?" Serj said.

Artan shrugged. "For what it's worth?"

"What's that supposed to mean?" the bald woman said.

"We'd be foolish to trust people we don't know."

The bald woman bristled where she sat, Collette resting a placating hand on her leg.

"We don't know yet," Serj said. "But we haven't given up. We'll find a way south, and when we get to the wall, we'll find our way over it."

"And you really think it's worth it?" William said.

The bald woman grinned. "Only one way to find out."

Jezebel on the grass beside him, William picked her up and got to his feet. The bald woman's right hand went to the knife at her hip. "Thank you for your hospitality," he said, "but we need to get going."

"Oh?" Collette said, her back straightening.

"We have to find Grandfather Jacks' community."

The nomads who had been standing guard all turned to face William. The wind howled across the open space. The fire fizzed and spat.

A tighter grip on Jezebel's handle, William's voice wavered. "He has two of our friends. Two girls about the same age as us. One of them is short and feisty. The other one a bit taller." He pointed at Artan. "She looks a lot like him. I don't suppose you've seen them, have you?"

"No." Collette shook her head. Although she answered too quickly for William's liking.

The bald woman snorted a laugh that made the fat around her neck ripple. "I'd give up on those girls if I were you."

"Thanks for the advice, woman—"

"Beatrice."

"*Beatrice?*"

"And if you shorten it to Bea, I'll cut your throat."

"You're a friendly one, aren't ya?" William said. "Well, *Beatrice*, Collette, Serj …" William looked at the others, twenty more of them; they all stared back. "Thank you for your hospitality, especially you, Bea."

Collette tugged on the woman's shoulder, pulling her back down when she tried to stand.

"We hope Artan's hunting skills have helped feed you all, but we need to get moving."

"Maybe you should stay for a while?" Collette said, her blue eyes narrowing.

William shook his head. "That's not a question, is it?"

Collette scratched her dirty face and pulled her matted hair behind her right ear. "There's certainly a path of least resistance before you."

Surrounded by nomads, Jezebel would do little for him right now. William lowered the double-headed battle-axe and sat back down cross-legged on the grass.

When Serj offered William another slice of meat, he pushed it away and spoke through gritted teeth. "No, thanks. I've suddenly lost my appetite."

CHAPTER 27

"Huh?" Olga said. "What? Has it stopped?"

A man stood before her. Broad shoulders, a scar up one side of his face, he held her muffs with both hands. When the babies were screaming and the lights blinking, she'd closed her eyes so tight the muscles along the sides of her head now spasmed.

Barp!

The light a constant, the man turned the muffs over in his shaking hands. "This is all part of your conditioning to make sure you're worthy of Grandfather Jacks' affection." His entire body trembled. He closed his eyes, pulled in a deep breath, and faced the ceiling. His words came out fast and loud, bouncing off the hard stone walls. "Praise be to Grandfather Jacks, the High Father, and his followers. Praise be to the great lord. To the provider."

When he opened his eyes, he spread them wide. They glowed as if invoking the name of a fictional god had invigorated him. He no longer shook. "We give thanks to the High Father for all he does. For our guidance, support, and nurturing. We love him like he loves us; we give ourselves over to him. We serve him how he needs us to serve him, and we thank him for his guidance."

Matilda watched on from her restraints, her lips tight, deep bags beneath her eyes.

It took for Olga to taste the salt of her own tears again to even realise she'd started crying. "When will you let us out of here?"

Barp!

The man's nostrils flared and he raised his eyebrows. He shook his head ten to twenty times before he dropped down onto the cold and damp floor. He removed his right boot and then his right sock. Back on his feet, his voice had grown louder and echoed in the small room. "How *dare* you interrupt my prayer." His voice whipped Olga rigid. "How dare you!"

He gagged her with his sweaty and pungent sock. Olga nearly choked on her excess saliva, damn near drowning in her nausea.

"You!" the man said, snapping forwards so his face stopped just inches from Olga. He then quietened and stepped back a pace. "Will listen." He nodded while splaying his fingers and stretching them back, bashing the heels of his palms together as if he had no control over the demented action. "Oh yes, you will listen. You will."

The rushing sound of water entered the room, but Olga couldn't place its source.

The man broke into prayer again. "Thank you, Grandfather Jacks, for showing me the way. For illuminating my path through this dark, dark world and providing me with all I need to survive. Thank you."

Water spread across the floor, the light catching the rippling surface. The man made a splash when he stamped his bare foot, his boot still in his hand. "Without you, I would have ended my life a long time ago. You've given me strength and purpose. You've given me a reason to go on."

As the water rose, Olga's pulse quickened. She'd never learned to swim. No one learned to swim in Edin.

Water kicked up around the man's feet when he crossed the room and stood in front of Matilda. "Do you give praise to the High Father?"

Barp!

Matilda stared straight at him.

The man moved so quickly, the sound registered with Olga before the slap. A red welt stood out on Matilda's cheek.

"You need more time," the man said. "Yes." He nodded. "You need more time."

Olga didn't need any more time, but she couldn't tell him. His filthy sock in her mouth reduced her words to muffles and stifled cries. Even the sloshing of the rising water against the walls spoke louder than her.

The man exited the room and left the door open. His words echoed in the corridor outside. "You need more time."

CHAPTER 28

Although William kept his map in his back pocket, he didn't need to check it to know they were heading in the wrong direction. But what could he say? He had no control here. His lungs tight, his breathing heavy, his legs tired, he pushed on through the long grass with his friends around him. The nomads encircled them and set the pace. He clung to Jezebel, but his weapon wouldn't help him. So outnumbered, they stood no chance in a fight.

Of the four of them, Artan kept the pace with the most ease. Fitter, faster, and probably stronger than all of them despite giving away nearly four years to William and Max, and two to Cyrus.

Cyrus struggled the most, his strides clumsy as if he might fall. He leaned closer to Max as they ran. "Are you okay?"

Max stared straight ahead, his face locked in his usual scowl.

It had been at least two hours since they'd eaten, and William had well and truly run off his stitch. Maybe the nomads had taken on less meat, because none of them appeared to struggle. Collette, Serj, and Beatrice closest to them, they ran as if they could go forever. And with their lifestyle it made sense. No good getting a stitch when you had to move at a moment's notice.

The dark grey sky grew darker as they ran into the evening. The long grass similar to that north of the funnel. They said life was easier in the north, but what did they know?

"What's that?" Cyrus said.

"What?" Serj said.

"That glow on the horizon."

It took for Cyrus to point it out for William to see it too.

"It's a community."

"Why's it glowing?"

"Electricity."

"What?"

"You don't have electricity in the north?"

Cyrus took a few seconds to catch his breath. "We saw a glass sun in Umbriel. That's the place where Grandfather Jacks' hunters live."

Serj laughed. "You lot from the north are a simple breed, eh?" He shook his head and laughed again. "Glass sun! It's called electricity. We can take power from the sun and turn it into things like light, heat, and sound."

"How?"

Serj shrugged.

"Why's there so much steel scattered around?" Cyrus said.

Beatrice sneered. "You're a nosey one, aren't you?"

"Inquisitive."

"I don't like inquisitive."

"You don't like much," William said. "I'm not sure

anyone should live their lives based on what you do and don't like."

Collette spoke before Beatrice could. "They brought all the steel up here to build the wall and ended up with more than they needed. It was too heavy to take back, so they left it. Sometimes people take it and melt it down, but most of the communities have used all they want already."

"It seems like quite a valuable resource to leave lying around," Cyrus said, his breaths becoming more ragged from trying to talk and run at the same time.

"To you maybe," Collette said.

"So when are you going to let us go?" William said.

Serj pulled his long hair away from his face, tucking one side and then the other behind his ears. The swish of the long grass against their legs, they maintained their pace. "This is for your own good, trust me."

Max's voice broke and grew louder. "And what about the girls we need to help? Is it for their good?"

"There can only be one winner between you and Grandfather Jacks," Serj said. "You need to accept we're saving your lives."

Beatrice sniggered. "And protecting our bounty."

Serj shot Beatrice a glare.

"What?" William said.

If Serj's wrath scared Beatrice, she hid it well. "We've seen your two girls. We took them to Grandfather Jacks."

Serj threw his arms up. "What are you getting from this, Beatrice?"

But the bald woman continued. "He paid us in deer meat and clothes. How will it look if we've taken his payment and then we let you lot get yourselves killed by going to his community? He'll ask us for a refund."

William lost his step, stumbling into a dip in the ground before regaining his balance. "You took the girls to him?"

Collette cut Beatrice off. "We do what we need to do to get paid."

"Even if it endangers your life?" Artan said.

While shaking her head, Collette, who maintained steady breathing despite running for as long as they had, said, "Grandfather Jacks isn't a threat to us."

"Maybe not directly," Artan said, "but your actions have put you all in danger."

"You think we should fear you?" Beatrice said. "An impotent rescue party. A band of boys playing at being men."

William's pulse quickened, his torso tense. He bit back his response. They were outnumbered. No matter what he thought of them and what he wanted to do, they were vastly outnumbered.

"At least tell us what he's like," Cyrus said. Although out of breath, the boy remained calm.

Serj shook his head. "We can't say anything."

For the second time, Beatrice showed her disregard for Serj's leadership. "He's as mad as a box of frogs." She smiled and winked at William. "He takes young women and girls, and because he's a Jaffa—"

"A what?" Max said.

"A Jaffa. He's seedless. He can't get women pregnant. He's convinced his community of nutters that it's a gift from the High Father; whoever the hell the High Father is. He says it's his job to break in the girls and young women for the sake of the tribe."

William caught Max's arm when he lunged for the bald woman. Although Max pulled against him at first, he finally accepted the restraint. William said, "So you think it's okay to give our friends over to that?"

Beatrice stopped running. Collette, Serj, and the surrounding nomads copied her.

William tightened his grip on Jezebel as he and the boys also halted. He wouldn't go down without a fight.

But they'd stopped for a different reason. The nomads at the front turned their backs on William and his friends and raised their spears.

Four or five diseased stumbled from around the side of a large lump of steel.

Artan moved so quick, William only saw his spear once he'd thrown it. It sailed through a small gap between two of the nomads at the front of the group and slammed into the face of one of the diseased.

The nomads took Artan's lead and dropped the others with well-aimed spear throws.

"You're quite adept with that thing, aren't ya?" Collette said. "You always need to be careful this side of the funnel. When you see one diseased, they might well be a part of a—"

One of the lead nomads turned to those behind him and cupped his mouth to amplify his voice. "Swarm!"

"Oh shit," Beatrice said.

For the first time since William had met her, the smug sneer fell from her face.

CHAPTER 29

The cold water reached Olga's chest, her tight bonds restricting her violent shivering. Her mouth still gagged with the rancid sock, she dragged desperate breaths in through her nose.

A surge ran through the water. A solitary wave, it lowered the level, dropping it to Olga's abdomen. Another surge, it dropped to her waist. Matilda had gone into a trance, her eyes unfocused and her lips pursed as she stared straight ahead.

Barp!

The water level dropped in stages, falling to just a few feet from the floor. The splash of steps outside hailed a visitor. A woman entered the room. Surgical in her approach, she removed the sock from Olga's mouth like a disinterested nurse pulling an old bandage off a wound far too insubstantial to be wasting her time with.

Olga's jaw trembled and she drew stuttered breaths.

"Do you give yourself over to Grandfather Jacks?"

Before Olga could get her words out, the woman tutted, her brow pinching. "You hesitated."

"W-w-w-wait," Olga said. "I'm cold. I'm t-t-trying to catch—"

"You. Hesitated." The woman shoved the sock back into Olga's mouth as if she wanted to break her teeth.

Barp!

Although Olga screamed, snot shooting from her nose, the woman had already turned her back and left the room. She hadn't even bothered to ask Matilda. Maybe they'd identified Olga as the one who needed to be broken. If only they'd given her a chance to tell them. She was ready. She'd do whatever they wanted.

The rushing sound of water filled the room again and the level slowly rose.

Matilda—strapped to her trolley the entire time—remained calm but distant. Wherever she'd gone, she'd left the room. If only Olga could go with her. Her straps restricting her trembling form, she fought to get a handle on her stuttering breaths. Her lungs were tight from where her nose failed to sate her need for oxygen. If only she could find even a shred of Matilda's calm.

CHAPTER 30

Collette showed the boys where she wanted them by motioning with the tip of her spear. "Get on that lump of steel over there." She then called to the group watching the swarm, "How long?"

A slim man stood at the front of the pack, his hair tied in a ponytail. He shielded his brow from the sun. "Two minutes at the most."

"I need rope." While one of the nomads ran off in response to Collette's request, Serj and Beatrice helped her shepherd the boys towards the lump of steel she'd set her sights on. "Now get on it."

Even with the distractions and many of the nomads readying for the oncoming swarm, the boys would get taken down in seconds if they fought back now. They climbed on the steel, William the last of the four to get on the large rock. About eight feet from the ground, the wide top of the steel lump had a plateau of about ten to fifteen feet square.

Collette, Serj, and Beatrice followed them up, Collette red-faced when she said, "You should be grateful we're showing you kindness." The nomad who'd run off at her request returned with a length of rope and handed it to her before moving off to join the pack watching the oncoming horde. Collette walked it around the boys before jumping down to the ground. Serj followed her while Beatrice tied the knot, biting down on her bottom lip with the effort of pulling it tight.

"Where are you going?" Cyrus said, his voice wavering. Whining.

Beatrice shoved him, and all four of the boys had to fight to maintain their balance. "Don't you worry about where we're going," she said, "just make sure you don't fall when the swarm arrive."

Cyrus squirmed where he stood. "But please. You can't leave us here."

"You're lucky we're leaving you here and not on the ground," Serj said. "Now wind your neck in."

But Cyrus didn't listen, his eyes glistening with the sheen of tears. He twisted and turned. "We're going to die out here."

"One minute," the slim nomad at the front of the pack called.

Beatrice tugged Jezebel from William's grip, the war hammer from Max's, Cyrus' sword, and Artan's knife and spears. She threw them into the long grass. "You can get them back when the swarm have passed."

"Come on," Cyrus whined. "Just let us go!"

The pitch of Cyrus' voice twisted tension through William's back. But Max spoke before he could. "Cyrus, if you don't shut the hell up, I'm going to drag all of us off this damn rock just so I don't have to listen to you anymore."

"Thirty seconds," the lookout shouted.

Collette and Serj ran towards a slimmer and shinier piece of steel nearby. It looked too narrow to stand on.

"Twenty seconds."

Beatrice reached into William's pocket and pulled out the hummingbird hair clip. "I wondered what this was."

"Give it back."

"Fifteen seconds."

Beatrice turned the clip over in her hands. "I like it."

"But you have no hair."

"Don't be so discriminatory." Beatrice jumped from the lump of steel and chased after the others. As she closed down on the slim and shiny rock, Serj shoved it over, revealing a hatch beneath. He kicked it open, revealing a tunnel he vanished into, the others following.

Half of the nomads had disappeared underground by the time the swarm's front runners appeared. Already hundreds of them, they were clumsy as they charged at a flat-out sprint.

"My god," Artan said. "And I thought Edin was bad."

The diseased screamed as if in an open challenge to the gods.

The hatch slammed shut as the one who'd given them a countdown on the approaching pack vanished into the hole.

"What do we do?" Cyrus said.

"Hold your ground." Artan shook his head. "They can't get to us up here. It's not like we haven't seen swarms of them before."

"Yeah," Cyrus said, "but not as many as this."

"Get a backbone, Cyrus," Max said. "Your whining's doing my head in."

They might not have been able to reach them, but it didn't prevent the diseased from slamming into the steel rock, shaking the wide lump. The vibrations ran through the soles of William's feet. More and more diseased appeared. There were thousands of them like Collette and Serj had said. Thousands upon thousands.

Cyrus shook so violently, it wobbled them all.

"Why were you begging them?" Max said. "What did you hope to achieve?"

After several rounds of damn near hyperventilation, Cyrus twisted his body and the rope fell loose, landing on the steel at their feet. He still shook, his voice wavering as he stared at his hands. "I was wedging my fingers in the rope so I could untie the knots when they left us. They had limited time, and I thought I could distract them so they didn't notice what I was doing with my hands." He dropped down and sat cross-legged. He pressed his palms against the solid steel surface. He squinted as he looked up at Max. "It's over to you now."

CHAPTER 31

"You poor, poor thing." The woman yanked the sock from Olga's mouth. She might have had kind words, but everything else about her screamed fury. At least six feet tall and as broad as any man Olga had met, she held herself with a locked tension as if it took all her strength to contain her rage.

The guard's old sock as soaked as the rest of her, Olga's tongue ached from where she'd pushed against the fabric of it to prevent herself choking. She'd swallowed more water filtered through it than she cared to think about. How long had the guard worn it before putting it in her mouth?

Someone stepped from around the larger woman and Olga gasped. "Heidi?"

The black-haired girl smiled. "We've come to get you out of here. I've assured them you're ready to meet Grandfather Jacks. That you're ready to join us in the ceremony tomorrow."

Olga nodded. "I am."

The woman who'd removed the gag said, "I'm not sure she is. She just hesitated."

"I didn't," Olga shouted.

A slight raise of her left eyebrow, the tone of the woman's voice dropped. "Watch yourself, girl."

"But I didn't hesitate."

Heidi stroked the woman's large arm. "She didn't." And then to Olga, "We're going to get both of you out of here. We're going to get you somewhere you can rest up so you're ready for tomorrow. I'm afraid we need to blindfold you."

Olga's heart quickened. "Why?"

"It's for your own good. There are things down here you don't want to see."

Matilda watched on, her lips pursed. The clarity had returned to her gaze.

The large woman discarded the old sock and pressed a blindfold across Olga's eyes. She snapped the knot at the back tight, but Olga stifled her cry. This woman seemed desperate for an excuse to lose her temper.

Olga tracked the two women by their footsteps as they crossed the room to Matilda. If the tying of the blindfold hurt her friend, she couldn't tell.

More steps entered the room. Olga's heart skipped when her trolley tilted back on its wheels.

Both being in a basement room and the sound of rushing water had muted the tone, but now they were out in the corridor, the bone-shuddering *barp* called as loud as ever.

A squeaky wheel on her trolley, everything aching, Olga pressed her tired eyes tightly shut, the forward motion and wobble going some small way towards easing her anxiety. At least they were going to get out of that damn room.

They came to a halt after several twists and turns. The large woman said, "Thank you, Heidi."

"Praise be to the High Father," Heidi said.

"Praise be."

Olga said, "Where's she going?"

The woman smelled of leather and dirt when she leaned close. She spoke in a low growl. "Never you mind."

They set off again. Where they were heading uphill before, they now travelled downhill.

"Where are you taking us?" Olga said. "Matilda, can you see?"

"No," Matilda said.

"Where are you taking us?"

They stopped again. Footsteps left the room. The large woman leaned close, sniffing Olga. "I love the smell of someone about to break. Someone who's soon to be pure enough to give themselves over to Grandfather Jacks. It reminds me of fresh rain on a summer's morning."

Rushing water entered the room.

Adrenaline drove Olga's words. "I'm pure enough now. I am. I'm ready. Please, I'm ready."

One more deep sniff, the woman said, "You hesitated." Her feet sloshed as she left the room.

CHAPTER 32

No matter how many times William had watched him do it, when Max dropped into the diseased crowd—especially a crowd as large as this—his heart accelerated.

Max shoved several diseased aside, clearing a space so he could retrieve their weapons. He first threw Jezebel up onto the steel rock and then Cyrus' sword before passing Artan his spear and knife. The diseased paid him no mind, their blood red eyes glistening in the fading light, their jaws working, chewing the air.

His war hammer over his shoulder, Max barged a path through the monsters. He shoved and pushed his way past, sending many of them stumbling away from him. Like he'd done with the weapons, he cleared a space around the hatch the nomads had vanished into. Yelling, he brought his hammer over and slammed it against the steel door of the nomads' shelter. It let out a loud hollow *tonk!* The door buckled from the first blow.

"They must have it locked from the inside," Cyrus said.

Max drove another swing at it. Another loud *tonk!*

After his third attack on the door, Max reached down,

pulling on a raised lip of the now buckled steel. A hand appeared from inside and Max quickly withdrew. The tip of a spear poked out next.

Max drove yet another blow against the doors, catching the end of the spear and snapping it clean off. He threw several more attacks, yelling louder than the diseased around him. Every blow buckled the steel barrier until he had enough of a lip to grab with both hands, setting his war hammer down in the process. He tore the door free and tossed it aside before retrieving his weapon.

Collette raised her head above the hole.

Max sank his hammer into her with a stomach-tightening *crunch!* He then jumped aside, allowing the diseased at his back to flood into the bunker.

The yells and cries of the soon to be diseased joined the already turned. Beatrice managed to poke her bald head from the hole before another surge of the vile creatures forced her back in. William smiled. "I bet she tastes bitter."

The reek of vinegar and rot curdled the air around them. William dragged in a deep breath before cupping his mouth with his hands. "Max, come back now."

But Max remained in front of the bunker as more and more diseased streamed in.

The nomads' cries died down. The diseased rush slowed. Many of them remained in the bunker, but those outside lost interest.

Cyrus sighed. "Do you think they're all gone?"

"I hope so," Artan said. And then he added, "What the hell's Max doing now? Max?"

But Max stared into the tunnel for a few seconds before shoving the diseased aside and climbing down into the hole.

William screwed up his face. "What the hell is he doing? I bet it stinks down there."

"Do you think he's finally lost it?" Artan said. "Those nomads might have been arseholes, but it can't have been easy to watch them die up close. What do you think, Cyrus? You've talked to him more than any of us."

"Hardly though," Cyrus said. "Although, he's clearly not been the same since Olga."

"We'll find the girls," Artan said. "He'll be able to make it up to her."

Cyrus nodded while holding his bottom lip in a pinch, his focus on the tunnel Max had descended into. "We will. And we know much more now than we did before. We know for sure the girls are with Grandfather Jacks. And we know the community is close. We'll get to them."

William spoke through a clenched jaw. "And we'll make Grandfather Jacks pay."

After a few minutes, Max emerged from the pit. He kept a tight grip on his war hammer, his entire body glistening with the blood and ooze of the diseased. His short hair matted with their mess, he walked with a weary slump, the red sky from the setting sun at his back.

The whites along the bottom of Max's eyes stood out as thick bands on his drawn face, his cheeks sallow, his skin pale. Had he finally lost the plot?

Max reached to William for a hand up, and for the briefest moment William hesitated. Artan then wrapped his arms around William's waist, anchoring him so he could pull Max onto the steel rock.

"Why did you go—" William noticed the hummingbird clip in Max's right hand. "You went down there for that?"

"It matters."

"It—" The words caught in William's throat and he nodded several times. "It does. Thank you."

"Welcome." Max sat beside Artan. "Besides, we have some time to kill, so why wouldn't I go down there?"

Both William and Artan sat down out of sight of the diseased. The fading light gave prominence to the glowing community on the horizon.

"It looks like we have quite a wait," Artan said. "But I suppose travelling at night is foolish anyway. Hopefully they'll be gone by the morning."

William lay down and held his left hand behind the back of his head. The hard surface offered little comfort, but at least the cold ran through his fingers rather than his skull. He turned the hummingbird clip over in his right hand. "I remember when Mum gave this to Matilda. National service felt like a big deal back then. Like our lives were finally starting. Who could have known it would prove to be so insignificant? Who could have known how many people we'd lose in such a short time?"

"I was expecting Matilda to breeze through it, come home, and get Mum and me somewhere safe," Artan said.

Cyrus said, "I expected to return to Woodwork to be with my nan. I thought she'd outlive everyone." He snorted a laugh. "Maybe she has. Maybe she's killing the diseased in Edin one at a time as she takes back her home."

"She sounds like someone we could do with now," William said.

Cyrus nodded. "She'd have Grandfather Jacks' head on a spike."

William growled, "So will I."

"I didn't expect a future when I left," Max said. "I thought our family's luck on national service had run out. I think I knew I wouldn't ever see my brothers again. But I thought that's because I'd be the one to die, not them. They were invincible."

Now they'd hidden from the creatures' line of sight, the moans and cries from the diseased had already died down. But they had a long wait before they could get off the rock. His body aching all over, the fingers in his left hand numb and cold, William let his head rest against the steel as he shoved his hands down his pants to warm them up. His whole body relaxing, his cheeks puffed out when he exhaled. "So much has changed in such a short time."

CHAPTER 33

Olga's clothes clung to her, her bones frigid from being submerged for a second time. She shivered as they wheeled her and Matilda into Grandfather Jacks' palace, the wind between the two buildings cutting into her, the morning sun burning her eyes. All the double doors opened before them, a gap parting down the centre, powered by an unseen force. Maybe electricity like Dianna had said. Who knew? Who cared?

A man pushed Olga's trolly while a woman steered Matilda. They wheeled them into the room they'd been in the previous day. Wooden pews on either side, the aisle led to an altar surrounded by cages. Heidi and the girl with the mousy-brown hair waited in one each. Heidi leaned against the bars containing her as if she'd collapse if she didn't have them for support. Had they brought her straight back here after she'd visited Olga and Matilda last night? The girl with mousy-brown hair stood spear straight in spite of her clearly broken ankle.

The man pushing Olga brought her to a halt directly in

front of an empty cage. The woman pushing Matilda did the same.

They loosened the leather strap on Olga's brow. She rolled her head to work some of the cramps from her neck. When they released the straps across her upper body, she fully filled her lungs for the first time in hours. They finally freed her legs. Olga moved forward with wobbly steps and entered the cage.

The man who'd pushed Olga's trolley sneered at her. *Crash!* He slammed her cage door shut. No way out from the inside; even opening it from the outside required a key.

Matilda looked across at Olga as if she expected something. But what could she say? They were done for. At least after this evening, after the ceremony and however long the man wanted them for, they could move on. Anything had to be better than nearly drowning for hours at a time.

The girl with the brown hair and broken leg grew giddy and hopped on the spot. The double doors at the end of the room opened. "Praise be to Grandfather Jacks."

Slim and over six feet tall, Grandfather Jacks wore a brown leather outback hat and walked with a slight stoop. Maybe as a young man he'd wanted to hide his height. Maybe he'd been bullied as a kid and didn't even realise he still tried to diminish his stature.

A gaggle of young boys from about eight to twelve years old gathered around him. Many of them had deep cuts and scars around their necks. A whip hung from Grandfather Jacks' belt, the end splayed, metal laced through the separate strips. No wonder the kids looked the way they did. No wonder Hawk was so angry.

Where Grandfather Jacks' eyes sparkled, his boys—his angels—wore the glassy stare of trauma.

"Olga," Matilda said, "we'll get out of this."

No more than fifteen feet separating Olga and Grandfather Jacks, Olga said, "Praise be to Grandfather Jacks. May he and the High Father look down on me and bestow me with his blessings."

Where glee had lit up Grandfather Jacks' features, he now positively radiated. A wide grin filled with wonky teeth stretching across his scraggly face. Striding straight up to Olga, he leaned against the bars while his angels held back. His breaths quickened to heavy pants as he looked her up and down, her sodden clothes leaving little to the imagination. "I like them small."

Olga ran her hands over her hips. "Small yet perfectly formed."

"Quite."

"I can't wait for tonight."

A smile so broad it damn near split the man's face in two. Grandfather Jacks scratched his grey stubble and continued to hold his chin while he nodded. "Very good," he said, looking from left to right along the cages. "I'd say all four of them are ready. Take them to my room now!"

CHAPTER 34

About halfway through the night, William had started shivering from lying on the steel rock, and he hadn't stopped since. His teeth chattering, he struggled to control the volume of his voice because of his quivering form. "It's a good job we didn't get left up here in the middle of winter. I'm not sure I would have survived." As he'd done most of the night—although less so over the past few hours as the sun rose, spreading at least the idea of warmth through him if not the reality—he rubbed his upper body to keep his circulation going.

Rolling over onto his front, William fished the map from his back pocket. It remained in the plastic sleeve, which had been effective at keeping it mostly dry. He unfolded it and spread it out on the grey rock. He pointed first to the depiction of Grandfather Jacks' community and then pointed off into the distance. "We need to head that way." Tugging on Max's leg to get the boy to crouch down beside him, he said, "How much longer do we have to wait?"

Max stood up again and looked back. Being invisible to the diseased afforded him that luxury. When he dropped back down, he said, "The bulk of the swarm can possibly still see us, but they are getting farther away."

"And at least they're going away from Grandfather Jacks' community," Cyrus said.

Max's demeanour had softened towards the boy. Cyrus might not be a fighter, but that didn't mean he didn't have value. He nodded. "It means the first bit's going to be the hardest, but once we're far enough away, we'll be able to put more and more distance between us and them."

"Do you think we can get away now?" William said.

Max frowned and raised his head. It took all William had to not sit up and look too. But if one of the creatures close by saw him, it could put them back by hours. Max got to his feet again and spun one hundred and eighty degrees to face where they needed to go before hunching down. "It won't be easy."

"What part of this process has been easy?"

"Fair enough." Lumps of steel littered the landscape. About fifty feet away sat a rock comparable in size to the one they lay on. Max pointed at it. "We should make that our first target. I think getting to that will be our biggest challenge." The swarm might have moved on, but there were still diseased scattered throughout their immediate vicinity. "If one of them sees us on the move, they could bring the lot of 'em back this way."

"And how much longer will we have to wait to be considerably safer?" William said.

"For these lot to go? And for the swarm to be completely out of sight?"

William nodded.

"A few more hours at least." Max then said, "If we're going to go now, I'll need to clear a path."

"I think we have to do it," William said.

"But"—Cyrus scratched his head—"if we alert the swarm again—"

"We might not get to Grandfather Jacks' community before the ceremony. I get it. But if we wait too much longer, we might not get there anyway. And the swarm are already far enough away to give us a good chance, right, Max?"

Max shrugged. "I'd say so."

"If it's a choice between going now or hoping things get better over the next few hours, when there's no telling whether they will or not, I say we go now." William shrugged. "And what if we don't, and then they turn around and come back this way?"

When neither Cyrus nor Artan replied, Max said, "I'll clear a path." The slightest hint of a smile lifted one side of his mouth as he jumped down from the rock, his war hammer raised and ready to be put to good use.

Other than their snuffling and snorting, the few remaining stragglers from the diseased swarm were quiet. Max walked among them like he belonged, a deep crunch every few seconds from where another beast yielded to a full-bodied swing.

∼

"We have to move now," Max said from the ground. "Let me chaperone you across. One at a time."

While lying on his belly, Artan freed a spear from where he'd tied several of them to his back. The knife he'd found at his hip, he felt for it before slipping from the rock and taking off at a sprint.

William released his tension with a long sigh when Matilda's brother climbed the rock fifty feet away.

"Who's next?" Max said.

William nodded for Cyrus to go.

"You sure?"

"Just go."

Like Artan had done, Cyrus armed himself. He drew his sword and slipped from the rock.

~

"Are you ready for this, William?" Max said, his face red from the exercise.

"As ready as I'll ever be. How's it looking down there?"

"The last two runs have been fine."

Jezebel in his hand, William brought his legs around in front of him and slid from the rock. A two-handed grip on the large axe's handle, he charged in the same direction as his friends.

Both Artan and Cyrus lifted their heads, fixing on William as he approached.

Although there were diseased's cries behind them from the gathered swarm, they were no more than their usual mutterings of discontent. The boys were too far away to be spotted by the main mob.

The rock in his sights, William fought for breath as he quickened his pace, his feet twisting and turning with the lumps and divots hidden beneath the long grass.

The air left William's lungs in a gasp when a diseased stumbled from around the back of the rock his friends were on. Blood red eyes, a slack jaw, and a canted stance. It fixed on William, its chest rising as it inhaled, its mouth wide, ready to release a call to the others.

William tightened his grip on Jezebel's handle, but he wouldn't get there in time.

A spear slammed into the creature's head, the flint tip bursting out the other side, dragging the diseased to the ground with its momentum.

His hand now empty of a weapon, Artan reached down for William, catching him and dragging him up onto the rock.

William belly-flopped onto the cold steel, but as he fought for breath, Artan on one side of him, Cyrus on the other, he put an arm around Matilda's brother and squeezed. "Thank you."

Artan smiled. "We'll get to them before the ceremony."

While nodding, William said, "I believe it. I really do."

CHAPTER 35

It had taken four guards to carry the cage Olga had been placed in to Grandfather Jacks' bedroom. Four had taken Matilda, four had taken Heidi, and four for the girl with the broken ankle. They could have all walked, even the girl with the broken ankle, which Olga had told them she'd happily do, but they'd insisted on carrying them.

Large windows—each one at least eight feet tall and four feet wide—ran along the side of the lavish room. Daylight flooded in, and even though they had Olga in a cage and she'd been in the room for hours, anything had to be better than the shadows deep inside the asylum. A four-poster bed in the centre of the room, it had cleaner sheets than she'd seen in a long time.

The automatic doors then opened with a *whoosh*. The tall man in the outback hat. Grandfather Jacks. The High Father by proxy. He strode in, a wonky grin on his stubbled face. Grey hair protruded from his wide leather hat, and he walked with an almost limp. Maybe the bulge in his trousers explained the awkward gait, although he more than likely was riddled with arthritis, his scrawny frame brittle and twisted.

Eyes only for Olga, his cheeks flushed. "The High Father has spoken to me," he said.

Olga pressed her hands together in prayer. "Praise be."

"He told me the formality of the ceremony, while important, shouldn't delay any longer what needs to happen. He's told me you shouldn't be made to wait. That I shouldn't deprive you." His words shook as if he struggled to contain his glee. "I should help you transition to womanhood today. You should receive your enlightenment now."

Again Olga pressed her hands together. "Praise be." Matilda's glare burned into her, but she refused to look at her friend.

Grandfather Jacks' hungry eyes ran the length of Olga's body. He liked them small. "Believe it or not," he said, batting the air with his right hand, "I'm old enough to be your true grandfather. I know I don't look it." The wrinkles at the side of his eyes spread with his forced smile.

A bulge in his right pocket, he reached into it and pulled out a bunch of keys. His gnarled hands shook as he fumbled to free her.

"Leave her alone," Matilda said, gripping the bars of her cage.

The old man's face twisted, the lust in his wide hazel eyes giving way to the intense focus of a predator. "What did you say, girl?"

"I think she's jealous," Olga said, reaching out from her cage and pulling on the man's sleeve, tugging him towards her. "She's jealous the High Father has picked me first. And you can't blame her for that, but don't let her ruin it. I'm sure she won't need to be told again."

Although Grandfather Jacks threw glances at Matilda, he finally unlocked Olga's cage.

Olga kicked the cage door with everything she had. With

the frustration of being bound. With the fury of them cutting Matilda. With the injustice of what had been done to Heidi and her friend. Of what he did to the little boys. The frame of the large door connected with the man's forehead with a loud *bang,* knocking him backwards, his arms windmilling as he stumbled away and fell to the ground.

Before he had a chance to get up, Olga sprang forwards and laid several blows into his old face, his hat falling from his head as she beat him unconscious.

The girl with the broken ankle shrieked, "Leave him alone!"

While Olga dragged the skinny man back to her cage, the girl with the mousy-brown hair continued. "She's hurting him. She's hurting Grandfather Jacks."

"Shut up!" Olga said.

"She's going to kill him. Help!"

The automatic doors had large handles that met in the middle when they were closed. Olga undid the belt around Grandfather Jacks' waist and pulled it free. She dragged the limp man and locked him in her cage before she ran to the double doors, tying the belt through them, bracing against them with her foot as she pulled the knot tight.

As Olga stepped away, the doors opened by just a few millimetres. Someone on the other side shouted, "We need help up here. They're hurting Grandfather Jacks. Come now."

Olga unlocked Matilda's cage, the door creaking.

"Well done," Matilda said.

Olga tilted her head to one side. "You knew I was faking it?"

"Of course. I was playing along. Not that I needed to, the stupid old fool is so full of himself, he didn't even suspect you were lying."

"Lust coupled with the male ego is an intoxicating mix, eh?"

The people on the other side of the door continued to hammer against it, and a blade slipped through the small gap. They moved it back and forth, sawing at the belt.

Matilda tugged Olga's arm. "Come on." She ran to the large window and threw it open, pulling a decorative knife from the wall and slipping it into her belt.

But instead of following her, Olga took the keys from Matilda's cage and delivered them to Heidi. The guards at the door had already sawed a deep cut into the belt.

Spears by the bed, Olga grabbed one. The girl with the brown hair screamed when she closed in on Grandfather Jacks.

Olga drove the tip of it deep into his right eye, a spasm snapping through the unconscious man before he fell limp once again.

"What have you done?" the girl cried. "Grandfather Jacks is dead. He's dead!"

The sword stopped sawing.

"Are you coming with us?" Olga said to Heidi.

Heidi shook her head. "I can't leave her."

"The girl you knew is long gone, sweetie."

"I can't leave her."

"Come on, Olga." Matilda already hung half out of the window.

The belt snapped. The doors spread open to reveal at least thirty of Grandfather Jacks' guards. Every one of them looked at their dead leader, the spear protruding from his ratty face. Had they focused on taking down Olga, that might have been the end for her. If she hesitated any longer, it certainly would be. Olga jumped up onto the window ledge and climbed out after Matilda.

CHAPTER 36

They'd been running for a couple of hours, yet William still checked behind for the swarm. For the first hour he justified it by telling the others the diseased were no longer following them. Now he kept that information to himself. There was only so many times he could give them the same newsflash. The run had driven the cold from his bones and loosened his frame.

They said little as they ran, other than: "We still on course?" Max said.

For what must have been the tenth time, William transferred Jezebel into a one-handed grip while he pulled the plastic-wrapped map from his back pocket and examined it. He turned it so it lined up with their environment, the imposing steel wall behind them. "Yep, it's all good."

"Wait a minute." Artan slowed down and the other boys copied him. "Who the hell's that?"

"And why's he alone?" Max said.

The man stood about the same height as Cyrus, the shortest of all of them at about five and a half feet tall. They had similar physiques, similar dark skin. As the man got closer, William squinted to see him better. The man had a young face and feline eyes. He could have been aged anywhere from twenty-five to fifty.

As they drew closer to one another, the man slowed down and smiled, his entire face lighting up, his eyes narrowing to slits. He led with his right hand and said, "Hi, I'm Peter."

"Where are you from?" Max said.

"I'm from a community in the deep south."

"Deep south where?" William said.

"Scringuard."

If only William knew more to challenge him on it. And he didn't want to reveal his map so he could check.

"Be careful," Cyrus said. "There's a swarm that way." He pointed back in the direction they'd come from. "A big one."

Peter nodded. "Thanks."

Cyrus then pointed over Peter's head. "How's the road back that way?"

"Fine. The diseased must have all gravitated to that swarm."

"And how far away is Scringuard?" William asked.

"Miles back that way."

"You've been running the whole time?"

"I have."

"You must be fit. You've barely broken a sweat."

"You have to be fit to stay alive out here."

William ran his tongue around the inside of his dry mouth. "Where are you going now?"

"North." Peter wiped his brow, dragging away non-existent sweat. "I've heard life's much easier up that way."

"I wouldn't say that," Artan said.

"Oh? Where are you from?"

Maybe William had recognised the man's face, and maybe the spear he carried at his back gave him away. But if he needed confirmation, it rested on the man's hip. He wore a knife similar to the one in Artan's hand. "You're one of the retired hunters."

Peter whipped his knife from his belt and widened his stance. His soft face sharpened and he raised his top lip in a snarl. "Just let me past, boys, and we won't have any trouble."

"Seems to me," William said, "that you're the one who needs to avoid trouble."

Peter slashed his knife through the air. "Let's see, shall we?"

CHAPTER 37

A steel guardrail ran around the edge of the palace's roof. A bar about an inch thick, it looked like a small fence. It stood about a foot tall. Exiting Grandfather Jacks' bedroom via the window, Olga grabbed it and pulled herself up onto the tiles, the rooftop of the large palace stretching away from them in both directions. The wind reminiscent of the funnel, it dragged loose strands of hair from Olga's ponytail and threw them into her eyes.

Barp! The tone from the asylum was much easier to hear now they were on the roof.

The patch of blood on Matilda's bandage had spread. "Are you okay to run with that?" Olga said.

Matilda spun the knife she'd taken from Grandfather Jacks' room and slipped it down the back of her trousers. "If I were you, I'd be more concerned with keeping up."

Wounded or not, Matilda had stepped into her element on the rooftops. She took off along the angled tiles as if she were running on a flat road.

No discussion about which way they should have gone, Olga chased after her friend.

Male voices called after them. Several hunters with spears had already climbed from other windows, and more were climbing out all the time. They might have been thirty to forty feet behind, but Olga recognised some of them. One of them the rookie hunter from Umbriel who'd won the first trial they'd witnessed. "We need to lose them, Matilda."

Matilda turned a sharp left and Olga followed. A spear shot past them. Had they not turned, it would have taken at least one of them down.

They moved faster than the hunters, opening up a lead with every passing second. Until—

"Shit!" Matilda stopped.

Olga's stomach lurched as she peered over the drop. At least twenty feet to the roof below. Too far to jump. "We can't turn back," Olga said.

The chink of a spear hit the tiled roof close to them.

Into a crouch, Matilda grabbed the guardrail and leaned over the edge. "There's a drainpipe here. It'll hold your weight. You go first."

"What about you?"

"I need to make sure they don't follow us. Now go."

It turned Olga's legs weak to lean over the edge of the roof. Thank god she had the guardrail. Hanging down from the thick bar, it took her a few seconds to find the chunky metal pipe with her feet. Adrenaline made her arms shake when she lowered herself. She dropped one hand down to catch the pipe. Rough with rust, she tugged it. It held fast.

"Hurry up, Olga." Matilda's voice had changed in pitch, her words quicker. A spear sailed above them before it landed with a clatter on the roof below.

Olga let go of the guardrail and dropped, halting her slide as she gripped the pipe with both hands. By the time she'd shimmied down a few feet, Matilda dropped over the edge and caught the pipe with barely a pause.

Fifteen feet to go, Olga slid quicker than before. The vibration from Matilda above ran through her tight grip.

A scratching of metal against metal, Matilda had stopped at the top of the pipe, the knife she'd taken from Grandfather Jacks' room in her hand. She used the pointed tip to dig into the wall surrounding the bolts that held the pipe in place.

No time to question it, Olga slid quicker than before. The rough and rusty surface burned her palms. She jumped off several feet from the bottom, the tiles cracking beneath her landing. A thick metal clip fell next to her. She jumped back in time to avoid the next one. The drainpipe leaned away from the wall at the top, Matilda hanging on.

The first hunter peered over the edge. "Matilda, they're on you."

About eight to ten feet down, Matilda detached the section of pipe she'd separated from the wall and dropped it onto the roof below. A hunter threw a spear at her and missed.

Olga hopped back another step, edging towards a bend in the roof that would take them away from there.

Still ten feet to fall, Matilda slid down the drainpipe and dismounted. She landed like a cat. She took off towards Olga, several more spears missing her as they smashed against the roof tiles.

Matilda caught up to Olga as she vanished around the corner. She spoke through heavy gasps. "That's bought us some time."

"But how much?" Olga said.

Matilda shrugged. "Hopefully enough."

CHAPTER 38

"Yeargh!" Max raised his hammer and charged towards the man, shoving William aside as he bore down on him. But before he reached him, Artan threw his knife. The blade sank into the man's throat.

A deep barking gasp, the retired hunter tore the knife free with a spray of claret. He clamped his hands to the wound and fell to his knees in the long grass. Blood escaped his grip, glistening on his hands.

It tightened William's chest to watch a man run out of breath. Not sympathy, just empathy for what looked like a violent and torturous end.

As the man's last strained gasp left him, Cyrus said, "What's that sound?"

Other than the wind, William heard nothing. "What sound?"

"Wait!" Cyrus raised a halting finger.

A deep bass note. It came from somewhere distant. It came from—

"That's where we're heading," Artan said.

Max still held his war hammer, desperate to use it. He

stood over the old hunter's corpse. "You think it has something to do with Grandfather Jacks' community?"

William bounced on his toes. "There's only one way to find out." He took off. "Come on."

Had the wind been blowing into their faces, they would have heard the noise much sooner. It took no more than five minutes for a giant industrial building to loom large on the horizon. "It's bigger than anything I've ever seen," William said.

The large structure cut an imposing silhouette. Tall and angular, it had square edges and towers of differing heights. A steel filigreed tunnel of gothic beauty led up to the place, which continued to belch the loud *barp* out into the landscape. It must have been louder on the other side.

Cyrus scratched his head. "Do you think that's Grandfather Jacks' place?"

"I think it's the asylum," William said.

While they were talking, Artan had walked away from them to the left so he could see past the large structure. "Hey," he called over the howling wind, "I think this might be his place, and I think I now understand what that noise is about."

William and the others joined Artan. Around the front of the industrial building, a horde had gathered. Thousands of them, nearly as many as in the swarm they'd encountered. "You think they're responding to the noise?"

"I'd assume so," Artan said. "Also, look at that building."

The diseased had taken all of William's attention. He'd not seen how the large and ugly building had not only blocked the horde, but it had also blocked the ornate structure on the other side. Unlike the asylum, the second building had plenty of windows and light brickwork. It might have been dwarfed by the larger and uglier building out here, but it was ten times the size of anything he'd seen in Edin.

Max, who still clung to his war hammer, said, "What if it's a trick?"

"Huh?" William said.

"To make people think he lives in the nice building when he actually lives in the nasty one."

Cyrus said, "The asylum does look much better protected than the smaller one."

"Do you think Grandfather Jacks is the kind of person to choose to live in that place?" William said.

But Max took the conversation in another direction. "Look over there! I don't believe it."

When William saw the boy, he said, "Shit! He made it here, then?" Hawk, armed with a spear, charged around the side of the asylum.

Max took off towards the boy, his hammer ready to be put to use.

When Hawk saw them approach, he raised a halting hand. "Wait!"

Artan readied his spear.

"He's mine!" Max yelled, still at full charge.

Hawk threw his own spear into the ground and lifted both hands above his head. "Please wait. You have to hear me out. I know where Olga and Matilda are."

The words took the pace from Max, allowing the others to catch him.

"What did you say?" William said while wringing Jezebel's handle.

"I know where Olga and Matilda are." Despite the strong wind, the grass swaying around them, Hawk stood semi-naked, seemingly unaffected by the cold. "You came here to rescue them, right?"

"How can we trust you?" Max said.

"You were lying at the bottom of that pit of dead diseased in the funnel, weren't you?"

"Huh?" Cyrus said.

"Why do you think I convinced the others the diseased had died when falling. I had to stop them being too curious. You didn't do a very good job hiding yourselves."

Max stepped closer to him. "You let us lie there for hours."

"I knew we needed to move on, but if I'd have been too pushy, it might have blown your cover. I left the deer meat behind on purpose. We never normally do that. And why do you think I gave Harvey a hard time about being able to piss in front of everyone?"

Max shrugged. "Because you're a dick."

"Because I saw you were already climbing out of the pit. I mean, you'd waited all night, what harm would it have done to have waited a little bit longer?"

Cyrus looked at his feet.

"If he'd have gone anywhere near the pit," Hawk said, "he would have seen you. When the others stopped in the cave to avoid the rain, I pretended they'd upset me so I could come back to keep you away. You were getting too close. It sounded like we were being followed by cattle. I don't know how the others didn't notice."

William stepped closer. "So why do all this for us? You hated us."

"Things change."

"Like what?" William said.

"Grandfather Jacks took Dianna. She's like a little sister to me. I never liked the man anyway, but at that point I had to question whose side I was on. I think we both want him dead. Once I get Dianna free from the asylum"—he held up a bunch of keys, the ring hanging from one of his fingers—"I'm going to track him down and cut his throat. I can't do anything about what he did to me as a child—" he rubbed the purple scars around his neck "—but I can make sure he doesn't do it to anyone else." His voice broke when he said, "Especially her."

Hawk wrapped his thick fist around the keys. "Now I can't stay here all day. Also, you need to hurry. Grandfather Jacks took the girls to his bedroom early. He normally waits until after the ceremony, but he's taken a shine to Olga—"

"He's not the only one," Max said.

"Let it go, Max," Artan said. "Olga kissed him, not the other way around."

"The girls are in his bedroom in the palace." Hawk said. "You need to get moving. We all do."

When Hawk ran in the direction of the asylum, William pointed at the palace. "So we're agreed?"

Max nodded. "Let's go." He led the charge.

CHAPTER 39

They'd stopped so Olga could catch her breath. "We're safe for now," she said, "but it won't be long before they find us again. We need to get the hell out of here." She shrugged. "But the second we go to ground, the guards will see us. There's nowhere to hide for miles."

Barp! They were now much closer to the asylum.

Matilda turned one way and then the other. "So where do we go?"

"I'm not sure." Olga pointed at the bandage on Matilda's thigh. It glistened with fresh blood. "And how much more running do you have in you?"

"Do I have to keep repeating myself? I've told you already; I'll keep up."

So far, Matilda had outrun her and then some. Maybe Olga should worry more about herself. But would Matilda really be able to get away from the palace in the open meadow with guards and hunters chasing them? Another loud tone from the asylum. Even from this distance, the sound snapped a shudder through Olga. How long had some of those girls been in that place for? How long had they had to listen to that torturous note? They set off again.

A section of the roof ran around what looked to be a courtyard in the centre of the old building. Like with every other part of the roof they'd come to, it had a sturdy guardrail running around the edge. It seemed like a waste of steel. What purpose could it have served? Regardless, it had more than come in handy for the girls. Olga led the way over to it.

"What are those things?" Matilda said when she joined her. "And why do they have diseased down there?"

The vast courtyard had over one hundred large black panels, each one at least six feet long by four feet wide. All of them were set at an angle of roughly forty-five degrees. Wires ran from them. "Do you remember what Dianna said about electricity?" Olga said. "She talked about something called solar panels."

"You think that's what these are?"

"What else could they be? It's certainly not Grandfather Jacks' connection to the High Father powering this place. And why else would they have diseased in the middle of the house? Surely it's designed to keep everyone away from this spot? He doesn't even want his guards out here looking too closely."

"But how's it going to help us?"

A set of double doors down to their right. A gate had been pulled across them, and a red light blinked near the handles. "Everything here is controlled by electricity," Olga said.

"So if we can destroy these, it will shut the place down?"

Olga shrugged. "Maybe? It's worth a try. It might be the distraction we need."

The *barp* from the asylum continued in the background, almost as if it counted down the seconds before another group of hunters found them.

Olga worked a roof tile free. The rough stone tore small stinging cuts into her hands. She held it like a plate and launched a spinning attack on one of the nearby panels. It hit the glass-fronted black sheet, a splash of cracks running away from the deep dent she'd driven into its centre.

Matilda copied Olga, both of them throwing tiles at the panels one after the other. Most hit, but some of them slammed into the screaming diseased. Those who hadn't noticed the girls at first soon spotted them. There were at least one hundred of the vile things, maybe more.

While Olga went one way around the courtyard, tearing tiles free and launching them at the panels, Matilda went the other and winced every time she bent down. Her thigh must have been worse than she let on. But what could they do about it in this moment?

The diseased ran from one side of the courtyard to the other, weaving through the sea of black panels. They looked like children playing a game. Furious children with bleeding eyes. They might have craved violence, but they had no way of sating their desire. Olga sent one in every five tiles into a diseased's face, nailing one of the creatures before she went back to destroying the solar panels.

The *barp* continued in the background.

When the girls met at the other side, every panel damaged in some way, Matilda pointed down at a metal box. Ten feet by six feet and four feet deep, it had wires leading from it back through the sea of black panels. "I think we might have to break that too." She pointed at the double doors with the gate across them. "That red light's still on. The electricity's still working." The tile she launched at the box shattered against the hard casing. It left a scratch but nothing more. "One of us needs to go down there."

"How's your thigh?" Olga said.

"Honestly?"

Had Olga not mouthed off in the cell, Matilda wouldn't have been cut in the first place. She stepped backwards so the diseased couldn't see her.

Matilda opened her mouth to speak, but Olga shook her head. Hobbling more than before, Matilda ran around the courtyard to the other side.

Olga planned her route to the box and back. It would be tricky, but there were enough window ledges to use as a step up to the guardrail. The drop no more than ten feet, she'd make it down there and back if she kept her wits.

A thumbs up from the other side, Matilda sat on the edge of the roof and hung her legs over the guardrail. Still several feet from the diseased, and definitely out of their reach, but the prospect proved too much for the creatures. The mob swarmed over, reaching up and shrieking, some of them slamming frustrated blows against the wall beneath her.

Reluctance locked Olga's frame. But what else could she do? They didn't have time to waste, and they had no chance of getting off the palace's roof and getting away from there unseen. This needed to end now. Her palms throbbing from the tens of cuts, she pulled another tile from the roof and slipped it down the back of her trousers before she too hung over the edge of the courtyard and dropped down.

A lock kept the box shut. A useless tug on the lid, it lifted a little way, but the lock resisted. The panels blocked her line of sight to the diseased, but the snarling, snapping, and rattling breaths were far enough away for her to work. Not that she could afford to be complacent.

A tight grip on the tile with both hands, Olga had one shot at this. She drove the edge of the tile hard against the lock. *Clang!* The bolt snapped. The diseased fell silent.

Olga crouched down behind the metal box. Maybe she should have run.

The diseased's snarls and shuffling feet came closer.

"Stay where you are," Matilda shouted. The wet squelch of tile hitting face, she yelled, "Come here, you dumb bastards."

The slow shuffle towards Olga halted.

Another wet squelch from where Matilda nailed another one. Olga jumped when a shard of tile hit the metal box close to her with a *ting*. Several diseased came to within a few feet. She saw the tops of their heads.

"Come on!" Matilda said. The clang of steel against brick. She must have torn one of the poles free from the edge of the roof, rapping the guardrail against the wall.

The creatures' fury reignited. They roared at the clouds as if they blamed the heavens for their current state. Olga held onto her tile. Not that it would help her against this lot.

Those close to Olga returned to the main pack, hypnotised by Matilda's noise.

"Go now, Olga."

Olga's hands shook as she lifted the metal box's lid. There were about thirty blocks inside. Whatever they were, they were clearly important. She reached in, grabbed a handful of wires, and tugged hard. She pulled again, disconnecting more and more with every tug.

Olga pulled the final few wires free, and Matilda continued to hammer against the wall with her steel pole. When she stood up, ice ran through her veins. There were hunters inside the building. Ten of them, maybe more. All of them watched her.

The red light by the double doors had gone off and they'd opened.

A diseased yelled. It had separated from the pack and blocked her escape.

Olga took off as the mob descended on her. Several hunters inside the palace ran away too. They must have been going to get help. She climbed up onto one of the solar panels, the angle shallow enough for her to scale. She leaped from one panel to the next, perching on the top of each one for a second before she moved on.

Olga drew close to Matilda. "Pass me the pole."

Ten feet between them, Matilda threw the large pole at her. Olga caught it, her stomach flipping as she nearly lost her balance. She moved from one panel to the next, closing in on the hunters standing on the other side of the cage in front of the open double doors.

Olga gained a small lead on the diseased. The densely packed panels forced them to take a weaving path after her. Many of them tripped in the cramped space, falling over one another. Olga had one chance at this.

The hunters on the other side of the cage poked their spears through the gaps as if they hoped for a shot at Olga. But as she jumped from the panels to the ground, she used her momentum and brought her pole down, snapping the flint tips from the wooden shafts.

Diseased's steps closed in. Olga raised the metal pole in both hands and drove one end down, stabbing it against the lock keeping the gate shut. It broke on her first attempt, the cage falling open before the hunters had time to grab it. She spun around and cracked the leading diseased in the face. Blood sprayed away from her blow and the creature fell.

A three-step climb out of there, Olga discarded her pole, jumped up onto a window ledge, shimmied up a drainpipe, and caught the guardrail, pulling herself back onto the roof before the diseased reached her.

Although some of the diseased followed Olga, many more saw their opportunity. Before the hunters could retrieve the gate and re-secure it, the diseased had rushed forward and overwhelmed them.

Some of the hunters flashed past the windows inside as they retreated from the horde, but many fell defending their position. The fallen quickly reanimated and turned on their own, overwhelming the hunters' weak defence.

The diseased cleared the courtyard. They flooded into the main building, adding to their numbers as they found more victims.

Matilda came to Olga's side and rubbed her back. "Well done."

Shrieks ran through the palace, and Olga pulled in a dry gulp. "Well, I'd say that's done it. Anyone down there is well and truly screwed."

CHAPTER 40

The boys closed in on the ostentatious building at a jog. Grandfather Jacks' palace. The second William met the man, he'd make good on his promise to cut his head off. Whatever happened, they'd get Matilda and Olga out of there, and they'd make that religious zealot pay.

The *barp* from the front of the asylum remained a constant until—

"It's stopped," Artan said. "I'm not sure that's a good thing."

While maintaining their pace, William shrugged. "You'd rather it continued?"

"No. I'm just saying the change might mean something. The fact I don't know what that something is, makes me uneasy. I'm sure I'm just being paranoid."

The long grass swished louder when Cyrus turned one way and then the other.

The asylum behind them, the large swarm it had called to its front remaining there for now, William quickened the pace. "Best we get away before they see us."

The two large doors at the front of Grandfather Jacks'

palace were wide open. "Shouldn't this place be locked down?" Cyrus said.

"Maybe Grandfather Jacks is so arrogant he doesn't fear for his safety," Max said.

William shook Jezebel once. "He's going to regret that."

A glass ceiling let in the sunlight, the bright glare reflecting off the highly polished white tiled floor. William remained at the front, running down one long corridor into a large room and then moving onto another corridor. Their footsteps echoed through the abandoned building. All the double doors were wide open. All the rooms they passed through were empty. "We need to find the stairs to get to his bedroom."

"That's if we trust what Hawk just told us," Max said.

Unlike every other set of doors they'd come to so far, the next set William arrived at were wooden and manually operated. They were split down the middle, and when he kicked them, they swung wide, each one connecting with the wall on the other side with a loud *crack!*

A large rectangular room, it had a wooden table dominating its centre with at least thirty places made for diners. Cupboards lined the long walls, six down each side, each of them at least ten feet tall. The ceiling stretched another few feet taller. The cupboards were loaded with serving equipment and crockery. Each of the long walls had a wide and shallow window running close to the ceiling. The table had been laid. They were to have a feast in here tonight. At least, it looked like that's what they'd planned. They weren't banking on William and the others turning up.

The doors at the other end were similar to the ones they'd burst through. Manual wooden doors, William charged at them. But before he'd gotten halfway across the room, they burst inwards. Hunters and what looked like maids and servants flooded in, their faces alive with panic.

William raised Jezebel, ready to fight, but the shriek of chaos on their tail stopped him dead and turned his blood cold. He looked over the heads of those charging towards him at the chasing pack. Maybe fifty diseased, maybe more.

"Max," William said, "can you take them down if we find somewhere safe?"

Before Max replied, William said, "Answer me, Max."

"Yes." He nodded and shook his war hammer. "Yes, I can."

To Artan and Cyrus, William said, "Get on the cupboards now."

"But what if they pull us off?" Cyrus said.

The first of the hunters flew past William and the others. "They won't. They're too high. And we have Max on our side."

Artan didn't need telling twice. Scaling the cupboard closest to him, he climbed on top and lay on his front.

Once Cyrus moved, William did the same, using the strong shelves as steps before he too lay on top of a cupboard, just a couple of feet between him and the ceiling.

Although Max climbed onto a cupboard too, he clearly wanted to bide his time and wait for the others to go before he revealed what he could do by clearing the room for them.

The first of the diseased entered the room riding on a maid's back. The woman screamed as she went down, blood spraying from where the beast bit into her right shoulder.

William's cupboard shook when a hunter tried to climb it. He kicked the shirtless boy in the face. The boy landed on his back, the diseased swarming over him.

The other cupboards were taken quickly, hunters and

servants of Grandfather Jacks finding their spots. Two to three of them jostled for space on some of the pieces of strong wooden furniture. If they were all like William's, they were attached to the wall with metal brackets, so they wouldn't fall easily.

Now they had to wait while the diseased tore down anyone in the palace who hadn't made it to safety. William took the time to catch his breath. Max would get them out of there, they just had to be patient.

A spear then crashed into the plates on William's cupboard, shattering the crockery. Another hunter launched one at Artan, who ducked at the last moment to avoid being hit.

"Shit!" William muttered. So much for being patient.

CHAPTER 41

Olga set the pace, jumping from the side of Grandfather Jacks' palace down to the long grassy meadow. Matilda followed a step behind her, her limp getting worse. "Are you okay?" Olga said.

While wincing and fighting for breaths, Matilda nodded several times. "I'm fine. It hurts and I need to rest, but that time will come."

The palace on their left, they headed towards the asylum. The tone now absent, Olga would have expected it to come as a relief, but the scores of diseased out the front now lacked the hypnotised pull towards the place. Many of them looked around as if trying to find somewhere else to direct their attention.

"Do you think the electricity's gone off in there too?" Matilda said.

A shake of her head, her face hot and sweating with the run, Olga said, "I hope not. It's bad enough in there as it is. We could really do with it not being pitch black too. I just want us to get in there, free all the prisoners, and get the hell away from this place." The crashing of breaking glass, tearing wood, and the screams of the diseased tore through the palace beside them. "And we need to get the prisoners out before the diseased find them."

They left the palace behind, the long grass whipping at Olga's thighs. At least five thousand diseased waited around the other side of the asylum. Without the tone, their attention could turn like the wind. If it blew the wrong way …

"Who's that?" Matilda pointed at the back of the asylum. A stocky and shirtless man exited the place, sprinting along the ornate steel tunnel.

Olga squinted to see better. "My god, it's—"

"Hawk!" Matilda said.

"Shit!" When they got closer to one another, Olga said, "What are you doing here?"

His large and exposed chest rose and fell with his heavy pants. The livid scars glistened on his sweating skin. "I've come to rescue Dianna."

"But I thought you were one of them?" Matilda said.

"I was. And I'm not proud of it, but something broke in me when Grandfather Jacks took her. It brought it all back. I used to be one of his angels …"

"One of the little boys he always has with him?" Olga said.

Hawk's blue stare intensified and his jaw widened from where he clenched it. "I hate him more than you can imagine, but he had a power over me that I couldn't get away from. And then he took Dianna." His voice broke and his lips buckled ever so slightly. "She's still so young. I won't let him do that to her. I won't let him do it to anyone else again."

"Well, you don't need to worry about that." Olga could still feel the crunch and squelch from where the tip of the spear sank into Grandfather Jacks' head. "Grandfather Jacks is gone."

"You're sure?"

"I did it myself. A spear through his face. I just wish I'd had the time to drag it out. I would have liked to spend days ending his life."

Hawk pointed down at Matilda's thigh. "What happened to your leg?"

"Don't worry about that." Although Matilda stood with her left heel raised as if to ease the burden on her thigh. "How is it in the asylum?"

"Dark," Hawk said. "The lights went out when the noise stopped. It's why I don't have Dianna with me right now."

"We need to get in there and free the rest of those prisoners."

"I know," Hawk said. "But with the place as it is, that could take hours. And if the diseased from the front of the asylum get wind of us being in there, we're never coming out again."

Olga placed her hands on her hips. "So you're saying we should leave them?"

"No," Hawk said. "I came here to free Dianna, and I will die doing that if I have to. I'd planned to come back out and pretend to be loyal to Grandfather Jacks until I found a better time to liberate her. I'm guessing now the best thing to do is to wait for the creatures to clear off and we can move freely in and out of the place. If that crowd get wind of us being inside the building, or if any of the prisoners leave any of the doors open, we're done for."

"Okay." Olga nodded. "It makes sense. So we find somewhere to wait it out."

"Where are the boys?" Hawk said.

"What?" Olga and Matilda said it at the same time.

Diseased's shrieks burst from around the side of the asylum. Just three of them, they headed towards the palace, slashing at the air in front of them, clumsy with their heavy steps. All three of them charged in through the open front doors.

Hawk said, "They went into the palace to find you both. I told them you were in Grandfather Jacks' bedroom."

"Shit!" Olga said.

"The palace has fallen," Matilda added.

"All the doors in the palace were electric," Olga said.

"So they're now all open?" Hawk said.

Olga nodded again. "Yeah. The boys definitely went in there?"

Hawk shrugged. "That's where I sent them."

"Shit!" Olga said again.

Twenty to thirty diseased appeared on the other side of the asylum, the side farthest away from them. One of them tripped and fell, but the rest maintained their rapid pace. "We need to get back to the palace," Matilda said. She took off with her limp. They had a lead on the diseased. Hopefully it would be enough.

The twenty to thirty quickly turned into hundreds as more and more of them came around the side of the asylum. How long would it be before it turned into thousands? Into a swarm moving through the landscape like a plague.

Olga and Hawk moved slower to allow Matilda to set the pace. She reached the side of the palace first. She might have been burdened by her limp, but she still knew how to climb, scurrying up the side of the building, showing the others a route to the roof. Olga followed, Hawk next.

Of the diseased who chased them, many entered the

palace. "We need to find the boys before the diseased do," Olga said. If they weren't too late already. Not that she spoke that thought aloud. She turned and led the others across the palace's roof towards Grandfather Jacks' bedroom. "I hope they've found somewhere safe."

CHAPTER 42

William called across the room to the hunters who'd tried to attack them, "Spears run out, have they?"

"You think you can do better with that axe?" The hunter who replied had the same shaved head as many of those from Umbriel. Naked from the waist up, he had a knife strapped to his hip much like the one Artan had picked up near the funnel.

While smiling, William shook his head. "No, actually I don't."

"So why are you grinning, you gormless fool?"

They had to shout to be heard over the hissing fury between them. Maybe sixty diseased were packed into the long room.

When William didn't reply, the hunter who'd been shouting at him reached down, retrieved a white plate from the top shelf of his cupboard, and threw it across the gap.

It fell short with a *crash!* "Max," he said, "we need to get out of here and find the girls."

Even over the noise from the diseased, the hunters' and

servants' gasps cut through the room when Max slipped down from his cupboard.

"How's he not getting bitten?" the hunter who'd argued with William said.

"More effective than an axe, spear, or plate, wouldn't you say?"

The vocal hunter shared his spot on top of his cupboard with another shirtless boy from Umbriel. As if for effect, Max stepped on one of the low-down shelves, boosted himself up, and pulled his friend off first. The boy screamed on his way down, the diseased smothering him in a writhing and hissing frenzy.

While kicking his legs in Max's direction, the first hunter drew his knife. "Leave me alone, you freak."

Max caught his right foot and tugged. He pulled so hard, he ripped the boy clean off the top of the cupboard and dragged him towards the middle of the room. The hunter's back made a gut-wrenching *crack* as he landed across the edge of the large wooden table, his winded gasp stolen from him as the furious diseased piled in.

"We don't want to fight you," one of the maids called from the other side of the room. "Please don't hurt us. We just want to survive this."

Three quick swings of his war hammer, Max cracked three diseased one after the other, dropping each one. "But the problem is," he said, "I need to keep my ability a secret, and at the end of the day, you *were* on Grandfather Jacks' side."

"Not through choice," the maid said. "You think we wanted him to do what he did to us?"

William tilted his head to one side. "Maybe you can't protect this secret forever, Max."

"That's easy for you to say. I know what this is worth. I've already paid the price for it, remember?"

Another hunter lay across another cupboard. Max dragged the screaming boy off like he had his friends, making his way down the room to the maid who'd pleaded for her life.

"Max—" but William lost his words when the doors they'd entered the room through opened with another *crack*.

More diseased burst in. They flooded the room like a plague. A swarm. If the stampede had an end, William couldn't see it. They headed for the maid closest to them, slamming into the cupboard she lay across.

The woman screamed and the cupboard creaked before collapsing, dropping her into the creatures' waiting grasp. Maybe the cupboards weren't as resilient as they looked.

A long and thin window along the top of each wall. It had been out of their reach, which hadn't been a problem until now. But maybe it would be the only way out of there.

"Max," Cyrus called, "help me."

Max shoved and barged his way over to the cupboard Cyrus lay on, attacking the diseased closest to it, stemming the flow as they tried to tear down the wooden shelves. "Pull back as much as you can."

Cyrus tucked into a ball, and the diseased stopped attacking.

"That's it," Max said. "They can't see you now."

His own cupboard shaking and rocking, the metal clip attaching it to the wall squeaking as if it could be persuaded to come loose, William did the same. But the top of his cupboard was too narrow for him to hide. The creatures continued doing their best to bring it crashing down.

The room filled, more diseased shoving their way in all the time. They were packed in so tight it limited their movement and made it harder for them to tear down the cupboards.

For now. But if they waited too long, there would only be one winner.

"We need a better plan, Max."

Max knocked down some of the diseased around Artan's cupboard before he headed over to William's.

"When you think of it—" Max grunted from the effort of crossing the room "—let me know. There's only so long I can keep this up."

CHAPTER 43

The girl with the broken ankle and Heidi remained in their cages in Grandfather Jacks' bedroom. They remained trapped, the cage doors locked. The corpse of Grandfather Jacks remained in the cage next to them. The spear remained protruding from his face. If only Olga had had longer with him. She would have skinned him alive.

But any rage she had for the man gave way to her grief for the girls. Heidi especially. It had taken her a while before she noticed Olga, Matilda, and Hawk at the window, but now she did, she fixed them with her crimson glare. She bit at the air between them, headbutting the cage as she lurched forward with each snapping bite. Blood coated her right arm, the deep red belching from the bite marks running all the way down it.

The other girl in the same diseased state, her ankle bent beneath her, her foot floppy. Olga shook her head, her weak voice cracking when she said, "We should have saved them."

"We didn't have time." Matilda pulled Olga away from the window and back out onto the roof. "Come on, all the diseased are downstairs. There must be something attracting their attention."

~

Matilda's limp did little to impair her ability to plot a route along the roof. They'd tracked the movement of the diseased from the outside, and when they came to one of the long windows, the pane covered in dirt, Olga rubbed a patch clear, her heart lifting. "There they are."

The dining room packed so tightly with diseased, Olga might have been able to run across the tops of their heads and not get bitten. Several tall cupboards along the other side of the room, the boys lay on top of them.

"How's he not turned?" Hawk said.

Max moved from one cupboard to the next, fighting back the diseased who threatened the stability of the tall pieces of furniture with his friends on. A lump swelled in Olga's throat. "He's immune."

"What?"

"It's a long, long story, and the reason he pushed me away from him in Umbriel. He's carrying the disease."

"Is that safe?" Hawk said.

"We don't know, which is why he's afraid of physical contact." Olga led them this time, climbing up over the roof to the window on the opposite side. A guardrail around the edge like every other roof on the palace, she shook it, rocking it back and forth, the steel creaking until the entire rail came off in her hands. After she shook the smaller bars free that had held it in place, she ended up with a two-inch-thick, ten-foot-long pole.

"What are you going to do with that?" Matilda said.

Leaning out over the edge of the wall, Olga slammed the

pole into the window with a loud *splash,* the cries of thousands of diseased bursting out of the room like a flock of spooked birds.

Hawk held Olga's hand, anchoring her so she could lean out farther to run the metal pole around the window frame to clear the jagged shards of glass. Unable to see him from her current position, but Olga knew where William lay. She shoved the pole in his general direction. "Here, take this."

"Olga?"

"And Matilda," Olga said. Best not tell them about Hawk just yet.

"William, remember how Max helped you get to us in the church when we got separated running away from Magma's community?"

"Yeah."

"Use this pole in the same way."

William took the pole, Olga and the others heading to the other window to watch him. He stretched it across to Artan, bridging the gap between their two cupboards. But instead of crossing, Artan took the pole and stretched it across to Cyrus.

Seconds seemed to last hours as Cyrus pulled away from the pole and shook his head. But Artan shoved it at him again. If he didn't take it and try to cross, he'd die.

Artan held the pole at one end while Max climbed the shelves and held it at the other. High enough to be clear of the diseased's reach, Max shoved Cyrus, who edged out onto the pole, swinging around so he hung down from it much like William had in the ruined city.

For a second, Cyrus clung on and froze. But after further encouragement from Max, he shimmied along the pole an inch or two at a time. The diseased tracked him from below, slashing at the air above them but unable to reach.

When Cyrus climbed onto Artan's cupboard, Max dropped down into the mob again.

"I'm not sure I'll ever be comfortable with seeing that," Hawk said.

Olga shook her head. "Me either."

Max climbed onto Artan's cupboard to help them stretch the pole across to William's. Cyrus led the way, climbing up onto William's cupboard before Artan followed.

Finally, the boys reached the pole across to the broken window. Olga and the others ran back over to the other side of the dining room. When Cyrus reached her, she took his hand and pulled him out, Matilda hugging the trembling boy.

Artan next, he climbed out of his own accord. He nodded at Olga, threw a sideways glance at Hawk, and then hugged his sister.

When William climbed out of the window, Olga said, "Good job you had a couple of women to come and rescue your arses, eh?"

William laughed, gripped either side of Olga's face in his rough hands, and kissed her forehead. "Thank you."

He approached Matilda and pulled something from his pocket. Tears stood in her eyes. They broke and ran down her face when he handed her the hummingbird clip. "I knew you were alive," William said. "I just knew it." They kissed.

Olga's heart pounded as she kneeled down on the roof and watched Max leave the dining room via the door. She stood up again and hugged the other boys one after the other.

∽

Despite everything they'd been through, Max finding his way onto the roof seemed to take the longest time. Cleaner than he should have been and in a new set of clothes he'd clearly picked up on his way out, his face glowed red and he avoided Olga's eye. "I had to get out of those stinking clothes."

Olga wrapped a hug around Max's middle. He locked his arms around her as he pulled her in tight. "I'm so sorry," she whispered. "I'm so sorry for how I behaved in Umbriel."

"So am I. I should have talked to you," Max said.

When she pulled away from him, her world blurred. But she still saw the tears also streaking his cheeks. She laughed and nodded. "Yes," she said. "Yes, you should have!"

CHAPTER 44

"It's beautiful, isn't it?" William said, his arm around Matilda as they watched the full moon.

Matilda nestled into his chest, her warmth enough to counter the bite in the air. The blankets Max had retrieved from inside the palace also helped.

Every muscle in William's body ached, but he couldn't sleep. Not yet. "We need to get your leg sorted out." He pulled the blanket away. The bandage glistened in the moonlight with fresh blood.

Her voice sleepy, Matilda said, "In the morning."

Hawk had chosen to sit farther away from the rest of the group, keeping watch for anyone else climbing onto the roof. Artan watched the other way, Cyrus at his side. The diseased had torn through the palace too fast for most, but they had to keep their wits. There were a lot of people in the palace; surely someone survived?

"We also need to find Dianna in the morning," Matilda said.

Olga and Max sat with one another, the full moon dusting them with a silver highlight.

The asylum cut an imposing silhouette. A reminder of the insanity waiting in the darkness inside. William kissed the top of Matilda's head. She'd closed her eyes, her breaths deep from where sleep dragged her under. He whispered, "In the morning." Although Max hadn't yet agreed to that course of action. And William couldn't blame him. He wouldn't want to enter the place on his own. Especially in the dark. Whatever happened, they'd find a way. But for now, they all needed to rest.

END OF BOOK SIX.

Thank you for reading *Three Days - Book six of Beyond These Walls.*

The Asylum - **Book seven is available now. Go to www.michaelrobertson.co.uk**

Support The Author

Dear reader, as an independent author I don't have the resources of a huge publisher. If you like my work and would like to see more from me in the future, there are two things you can do to help: leaving a review, and a word-of-mouth referral.

Releasing a book takes many hours and hundreds of dollars. I love to write, and would love to continue to do so. All I ask is that you leave an Amazon review. It shows other readers that you've enjoyed the book and will encourage them to give it a try too. The review can be just one sentence, or as long as you like.

THE ASYLUM: BOOK SEVEN OF BEYOND THESE WALLS - CHAPTER ONE

William woke up shivering. That had happened a lot lately. The familiar damp press of dew-soaked clothes lay against his skin, his chest frigid, the cool moist night boring into his lungs. He drew a deep breath and coughed with a phlegmy rattle. But at least they'd woken to a new day. At least they were moving into spring, and at least he had Matilda by his side. They'd fallen asleep in each other's arms, but she now sat up, her knees pulled into her chest as she stared out across the wastelands.

Maybe he should have lain there for longer. His body ached from head to toe, and he groaned as he sat up beside her. Her face pale, her brow beaded with what appeared to be dew, he reached across and wiped the moisture away, pausing on her hot forehead. "You're sweating, Tilly."

Matilda pulled her bandage away to show him.

A slow writhe turned through William. The wound, at least an inch deep and eight inches long, now glistened with a milky white pus. "How's it gotten so infected so quickly?"

Matilda shrugged. "Maybe they'd coated the blade with something. Maybe it was just dirty." Bags bulged beneath her glazed brown eyes. She continued to stare out across the grassy meadow, thousands of diseased below them. "And it's not like we can go on a hunt for ointment."

"How fast can you run right now?"

"I'm not sure. But I can feel myself getting slower by the minute."

"Shit!"

"And if I get any diseased blood in it …"

"We're screwed," William said.

"*I'm* screwed."

"There has to be a way to fix it. There's always a way."

Matilda's full lips thinned from where she pressed them tight. Her brow wrinkled. Positive affirmations were awful painkillers.

Olga and Max were stirring. They'd spent the night close, albeit with their backs to one another. They'd work it out with time.

Hawk had remained on guard on one side of their camp, Cyrus and Artan on the other. They were still staring out across the roof. Had any of them slept?

Hawk approached them. He remained naked from the waist up, his body tight with his bulging muscles. Deep scars slashed across his torso. He wore his wounds like a badge of honour. Just look at how damn tough he was. Although he put William to shame, who continued to shiver while the hunter stood impervious to the cold. As he drew closer, Hawk fixed on the wound on Matilda's thigh. A slight wince narrowed his eyes. The jangle of keys, he reached into his pocket and held up a thick ring on the end of his right index finger. "I need to find a way to get Dianna out of the asylum."

"You have just looked at the cut on Matilda's leg, right?" William said.

Another slight wince, Hawk then pointed at the large

industrial building on the other side of the sea of diseased. "Dianna's in that place. I need to get her out."

After working his jaw, chewing the air in front of him, William said, "Allow me to explain myself more clearly. Screw Dianna."

Hawk's muscles tensed.

"We wouldn't be in this mess if it wasn't for you and your fucked-up community of sycophants and alpha males. You'll forgive us for not prioritising your needs and the needs of those affiliated with Grandfather Jacks."

"Dianna's done nothing wrong."

"Neither's Matilda."

"I can speak for myself, William," Matilda said.

"Then why don't you?"

"I have nothing to say."

"Also"—William leaned to the left to look past Hawk at the asylum—"have you seen the state of that place?"

"It was bad enough with the lights on in there," Matilda said. "It must be hell on earth in the darkness."

"We need to make the best choices for us right now," William said.

"And what about Dianna?" Hawk's pecs twitched and his biceps bulged. Although he spoke with a quiet tone, a low thunder rumbled beneath his words. "She's a victim in all this too. As are the other women in there. You've been inside the place, Matilda."

As pale as ever, still drenched in sweat, Matilda dropped her focus to her lap.

"And what about all the children?"

"Children?" William said.

"The little boys." Hawk's voice wavered while he ran his fingers along the rope burns on his neck. He then traced some of the deeper slashes on his chest and shoulders. An involuntary reaction, his fingers relived the memories of his own suffering like a blind person reading Braille. "His *angels*. How will they fare with the dark insanity inside that place? The screaming, the cold, the damp, that damn noise calling the diseased to the front of the place."

"At least that's stopped," William said.

Hawk shrugged. "Don't you care?"

"I care very much. I care about what's going to happen to Matilda because of what she's been through. I empathise with Dianna and the others, but I'm sorry, they're not my priority."

"William's right." Max had moved closer to the boys. He stood with his feet planted, his legs wide to give him a strong base. He held his war hammer across his front with both hands and glared at the scarred hunter. "Hawk, you've caused this group nothing but trouble since we met you."

"*I* kissed him, Max," Olga said, "not the other way around."

The twist of Max's features ran counter to his words. "You think I give a shit about a pathetic kiss between you two?"

Olga's face reddened. Where she usually fought everything, she stepped back as if shoved by his words.

"You weren't there when we were out hunting," Max said. "When he handed us over to Magma."

Artan and Cyrus joined the group.

Max continued. "It might have done us a favour if you were. You might have been able to keep him distracted so he didn't send us to our death."

"I'm sorry about that," Hawk said. "I wasn't thinking straight." Again he rubbed his neck and chest. "Sometimes I don't think straight."

"Forgive me, Hawk," William said, "but if you can't take

responsibility for your own thoughts, how do you expect us to risk our lives helping you?"

"Helping *Dianna*!"

Max clenched his fists at his sides and stepped closer. He bared his teeth when he spoke, his face red. "You're lucky I don't throw you from this roof right now."

"Why don't you?" Another ripple of tensing muscles ran across Hawk's torso. "You'd be doing me a favour. I'm better turned into one of them than standing up here knowing Dianna's suffering and there's nothing I can do to help her."

"If you're so worried about Dianna," Max said, "why did you leave her in there?"

"It's dark enough in that place with the lights on." Hawk's eyes lost focus. "When the power went, the place turned pitch black. I couldn't see a thing. Also, when that damn sound stopped, what was keeping the diseased around the front of the asylum? At some point they were bound to get bored, and … well …" He swept his hand out over the wastelands.

"So you were scared?"

"Worse than scared," Hawk said. "The lack of electricity rendered me utterly impotent. If I waited too long, I would have also been trapped."

"It's bad in there, Max." Olga touched his shoulder, but he pulled away from her. "It was hell with the lights on. I can't even imagine what Dianna's having to go through now. She could be tied up. She might be submerged in water. She has no one to let her out. No one to feed her."

"Why do you care so much?" Max said.

"Dianna was kind to us."

William's stomach sank when Matilda nodded along with Olga. "She untied us when we were bound and helped us understand what we were facing. Without her warnings, I'm not sure we would have gotten out of there."

Max stepped away from Olga's touch, her hand falling limp at her side with a gentle slap. He moved a step closer to Hawk. No more than two feet separated the boys. Max stood as the taller of the two, although Hawk had pecs like rocks and biceps like baseballs.

The size of the boy didn't deter Max. He put his war hammer down so the head of it rested on the tiles. He removed his top. "Max," William said, "what are you doing? Put your clothes back on, man."

Max scrunched his top into a ball and threw it at Hawk. It hit the boy's wide, scarred chest and fell to the tiles. Instead of watching it, Hawk remained fixed on Max, the sides of his face widening from the tight clench of his jaw.

"You're not a hunter anymore," Max sneered. "You look ridiculous."

Another shimmering wave of tension rippled through Hawk's upper body at Max moving closer. He remained statue still, his glare unwavering when Max pulled the keys from his hand. He turned his back on the boy and stormed off.

"What are you doing?" Olga said.

"Going to the asylum."

Although Olga opened her mouth, she said nothing.

Without looking back, Max jumped down to a lower part of the roof. William stood up and followed the boy, watching his back as he climbed from the roof into the meadow filled with diseased.

Twenty to thirty feet away from the palace, Max spun around at the scream bursting from the building.

Four people emerged: one woman and three men. Hunters by the look of it, the men naked from the waist up. They charged Max, their weapons raised as they yelled fury at him.

If anything, Max's grip on his hammer eased and his

shoulders relaxed. He slowly shook his head at his approaching attackers and lowered his weapon.

The diseased slammed into them from all sides, hitting them hard and piling on top of them as they went down. Snarls drowned out the screams. Blood sprayed away from the palace's escapees.

"What were they thinking?" Hawk said.

William shook his head at the stocky boy. "They must have thought they could move through the diseased like Max."

"Why?"

"I'm not sure that's the right question."

"What is, then?"

After taking down a diseased and stealing their top, Max jogged towards the asylum. William tapped the tiles beneath him with his toe. "How many more of them are below us right now? At least the diseased are predictable, and there's no chance of them climbing up onto the roof. What if we're outnumbered by survivors too?"

Hawk stood as dumbstruck as Olga, his mouth slightly open as if the thought of a reply lay on his tongue. William nodded back at the scrunched-up shirt he'd left behind. "Are you going to wear that top?"

Hawk shook his head.

Retrieving Max's shirt, William sat down next to Matilda. Even in the short time they'd been awake, she seemed to have turned paler. Her skin a light shade of green, the sun hit her sweating face like it hit the dew-soaked grass. Holding the shirt up and then turning it around to show her the back, he said, "I'm going to wrap this around your leg. It's cleaner than that other bandage."

While biting on her bottom lip, Matilda breathed through

her nose as if even the thought of dressing her wound caused her pain.

William's hands shook as he swaddled her thigh. What if they couldn't find an ointment to deal with the infection?

Thank you for reading Chapter One of The Asylum - *Book seven of Beyond These Walls.*

The entire book is available now. Go to www.michaelrobertson.co.uk

ABOUT THE AUTHOR

Like most children born in the seventies, Michael grew up with Star Wars in his life, along with other great stories like Labyrinth, The Neverending Story, and as he grew older, the Alien franchise. An obsessive watcher of movies and consumer of stories, he found his mind wandering to stories of his own.

Those stories had to come out.

He hopes you enjoy reading his work as much as he does creating it.

Contact
www.michaelrobertson.co.uk
subscribers@michaelrobertson.co.uk

READER GROUP

Join my reader group for all my latest releases and special offers. You'll also receive these four FREE books. You can unsubscribe at any time.

Go to www.michaelrobertson.co.uk

THE ARENA
MICHAEL ROBERTSON

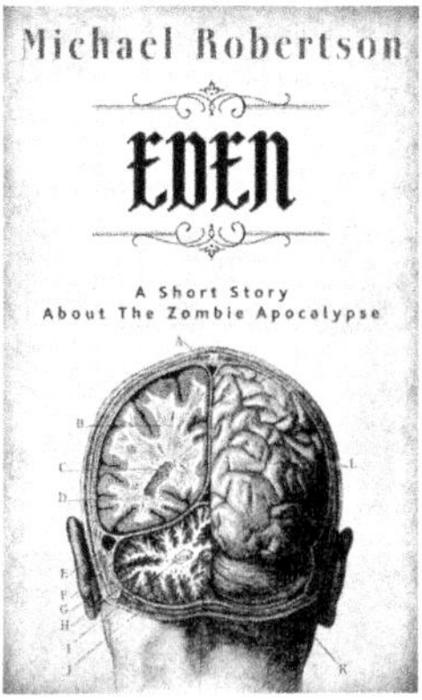
Michael Robertson
EDEN
A Short Story
About The Zombie Apocalypse

RAT RUN
A POST-APOCALYPTIC TALE
Michael Robertson

ALSO BY MICHAEL ROBERTSON

THE SHADOW ORDER:

The Shadow Order

The First Mission - Book Two of The Shadow Order

The Crimson War - Book Three of The Shadow Order

Eradication - Book Four of The Shadow Order

Fugitive - Book Five of The Shadow Order

Enigma - Book Six of The Shadow Order

Prophecy - Book Seven of The Shadow Order

The Faradis - Book Eight of The Shadow Order

The Complete Shadow Order Box Set - Books 1 - 8

∾

GALACTIC TERROR:

Galactic Terror: A Space Opera

Galactic Retribution - A Space Opera - Galactic Terror Book Two

∾

NEON HORIZON:

The Blind Spot - A Cyberpunk Thriller - Neon Horizon Book One.

Prime City - A Cyberpunk Thriller - Neon Horizon Book Two.

Bounty Hunter - A Cyberpunk Thriller - Neon Horizon Book Three.

Connection - A Cyberpunk Thriller - Neon Horizon Book Four.

Reunion - A Cyberpunk Thriller - Neon Horizon Book Five.

Eight Ways to Kill a Rat - A Cyberpunk Thriller - Neon Horizon Book Six.

Neon Horizon - Books 1 - 3 Box Set - A Cyberpunk Thriller.

∼

THE ALPHA PLAGUE:

The Alpha Plague: A Post-Apocalyptic Action Thriller

The Alpha Plague 2

The Alpha Plague 3

The Alpha Plague 4

The Alpha Plague 5

The Alpha Plague 6

The Alpha Plague 7

The Alpha Plague 8

The Complete Alpha Plague Box Set - Books 1 - 8

∼

BEYOND THESE WALLS:

Protectors - Book one of Beyond These Walls

National Service - Book two of Beyond These Walls

Retribution - Book three of Beyond These Walls

Collapse - Book four of Beyond These Walls

After Edin - Book five of Beyond These Walls

Three Days - Book six of Beyond These Walls

The Asylum - Book seven of Beyond These Walls

Between Fury and Fear - Book eight of Beyond These Walls

Before the Dawn - Book nine of Beyond These Walls

The Wall - Book ten of Beyond These Walls

Divided - Book eleven of Beyond These Walls

Escape - Book twelve of Beyond These Walls

It Only Takes One - Book thirteen of Beyond These Walls

Trapped - Book fourteen of Beyond These Walls

This World of Corpses - Book fifteen of Beyond These Walls

Blackout - Book sixteen of Beyond These Walls

Beyond These Walls - Books 1 - 6 Box Set

Beyond These Walls - Books 7 - 9 Box Set

Beyond These Walls - Books 10 - 12 Box Set

Beyond These Walls - Books 13 - 15 Box Set

∼

OFF-KILTER TALES:

The Girl in the Woods - A Ghost's Story - Off-Kilter Tales Book One

Rat Run - A Post-Apocalyptic Tale - Off-Kilter Tales Book Two

∼

Masked - A Psychological Horror

∼

CRASH:

Crash - A Dark Post-Apocalyptic Tale

Crash II: Highrise Hell

Crash III: There's No Place Like Home

Crash IV: Run Free

Crash V: The Final Showdown

∽

NEW REALITY:

New Reality: Truth

New Reality 2: Justice

New Reality 3: Fear

∽

Audiobooks:

CLICK HERE TO VIEW MY FULL AUDIOBOOK LIBRARY.

Printed in Great Britain
by Amazon